EVIL
LURKS
IN THE
DARK

THE ADIRONDACK WITCH

BESTSELLING HORROR AUTHOR
PATRICK REUMAN

The Adirondack Witch

No part of this publication may be reproduced, stored in a retrieval system, or transmitted in any way by any means, electronic, mechanical, photocopy, recording, or otherwise, without the prior permission of the author except as provided by USA copyright law.

This novel is a work of fiction. Names, descriptions, entities, and incidents included in the story are products of the author's imagination. Any resemblance to actual persons, events, and entities is entirely coincidental.

Cover design by Matt Seff Barnes
All rights reserved. Copyright © 2022 Patrick Reuman
All rights reserved.

The Adirondack Witch

A Patrick Reuman Novel

Dedication:

This novel is dedicated to the readers, as always, whose nightmares I wish to dwell in and call home. I hope you enjoy reading this novel just as much as I loved writing it.

The Adirondack Witch

Chapter 1

Hank sat in front of his keyboard staring at the empty bar in the chat as the vertical line blinked at him. Two cold, tall cups of iced coffee stood alongside him on his desk, one for him, one for someone else. He wasn't sure what kind of coffee she enjoyed, so he'd just went with caramel. Everybody liked caramel, he hoped.

He clicked on the chat bar and started to type.

It was five months earlier, in August, when she had first messaged him. It was an accident, really. The boss had sent out a group message in the company chat about a Christmas party they were having a few months later. Mary, being apparently unable to work technology, accidentally replied to him instead of the entire group. He responded back, and that was how it all began. One message turned into two, then three, until the two of them casually messaged at least once a day for days on end. Even though their conversations were about almost nothing, and they had never met officially in person, he cherished them, looking forward to reading her words each day when he arrived to work.

He stood outside the office doors, dressed in the nicest suit he had, the only suit he had, actually, wondering if he had overdressed for the occasion. Sweat rimmed his hairline and threatened everywhere else. He could turn back now, say he wasn't feeling well, or pretend he had fallen asleep early. Nobody would question it. Few would care.

Except this may be his only chance to meet her, to meet Mary Hawkins, the girl behind the conversations. He stepped through the doorway, taking in the office space as he did so. He recognized many of them, John, Sierra, Isaac, and others. Isaac noticed his entry and waved. Hank waved back, faking a smile as his friend signaled him over.

They greeted each other, then talked for a moment, mostly Isaac to him about how boring the party was and how he should have stayed home. All the while, Hank was keeping an eye out for a woman, a woman who he didn't even know what she looked like. He was hoping he would somehow just…know.

And he did. Nearly a half hour later, a woman entered through the same door he did, looking around nervously just as he had. He turned away from Isaac mid-sentence and walked toward the woman, making it mostly across the room before stopping awkwardly. He hadn't a clue what he was supposed to say, yet there he was, feet from her, as she removed her coat and hung it on the rack.

She turned to him before he could decide to make a run for it, nearly bumping into him, and greeted him with the most beautiful smile. "Oh! Hello! I'm a little late, it looks like." She looked around the room, at all the people, hesitantly.

"Yes. Yes." He stuttered a little. "But you haven't missed much of anything. It's a little boring, actually."

Her smile came back to life, beaming at him. "I don't think I've met you. Did you just start here?" she asked.

"No. Uhm. I've worked here for a little while now, since July."

Her face lit up. "I started in July, too!"

He knew this, or he was pretty sure of it at least, if this girl was who he thought she was. When she walked in, something pulled him toward her; something divine or magical told him it was her. No one else could possibly be that beautiful, after all. He tried hard not to start blushing.

"Mary?" Hank said, feigning surprise.

She narrowed her eyes. "Hank?"

Her smile spread to him. He could no longer contain the excitement he had been feeling since seeing her enter.

"I thought you might be here," he said. "But I wasn't sure."

"Well, you said you would be here." They were the first awkwardly spoken words to come from her, her words reflecting exactly how he felt. "So I thought I would stop by and say hello."

I found your coffee, if you want to come get it, he typed. He hovered his finger over the button for a long second before clicking enter and sending the message.

He waited.

And waited.

Then, finally, the computer told him that she was typing. He smiled wide as the words came up on the screen. She said she would meet him at lunch to get it.

Hank shot to attention, awoken by a loud ring blistering his eardrums. He looked at the phone as if it were a foreign object, as if he had no idea that picking it up from the receiver would halt the infernal screeching. He didn't care. His boss could walk by and ask why he wasn't doing his job and he wouldn't move. In fact, he hoped the sorry bastard did just that. Fuck him. And fuck his job. He would only be so lucky to get canned from this pathetic dead-end excuse of a life-drainer. He wasn't sure why he even came anyway. There really was no point, not anymore.

He jumped forward, snatching the phone up from its receiver. "Hello, this is Hank, how can I help you fix your shitty internet?"

He was greeted by silence on the other end, then a yippy dog barking. There was breathing, too, only it was so quiet he could hardly hear it at all.

"I—" a small voice started. "My internet isn't working."

Small, minute seconds of silence ticked by.

"It's not connecting at all," the voice continued.

Hank pulled the phone away from his head and looked at it as if checking if it were still a phone or if it had changed into something else entirely. Then, without another word to the squirrely woman on the line, he hung up the phone. He stared at the screen in front of him with its designated lines, which were supposed to be filled in with the caller's information in order to bring up their account info, and felt truly empty inside.

He stood, turned away from his desk, and walked for the door. Some others looked up at him as he went by, but he didn't care. Never in his life had he cared less than he did right then.

A wave of afternoon heat hit him as he exited the air-conditioned office building. The sun was high in the sky and mercilessly bright. When he reached his car and opened the door, an even uglier wave of hot, musty air rushed out to meet him. He plopped down in the driver's seat and started the engine, rolling down the windows right away even though he only lived a few minutes from the office. That was one of the reasons he stayed working there for so long. It was close to home, and home was close to where Mary worked, and Mary's job as a head advertiser for a locally headquartered beverage company was a much higher-paying gig than his was.

But Mary was dead now. And the seat where she always sat alongside him in their car was empty, the floor below it covered in various fast-food wrappers and napkins. That's what smelled so bad. He already knew this. But he didn't care.

He put the vehicle into gear and pulled out from the parking lot. Only a few streets away, he arrived back at his now-too-big house. He didn't remember the short trip at all. He had been on autopilot, just as he often was those days, thinking about nothing at all.

He walked up the white steps toward the mahogany door that Mary had picked out because she didn't like the black door that had been there before. He hadn't cared about what color the door was, so he let her do as she wished with it. Most of the house was this way. That's why everything was so painful now. Everything, every square inch of his house, was touched in some way by Mary.

Silence. Complete and utter silence was all that he found on the other side of the mahogany door. It was the same thing that greeted him every other day when he arrived home. And so, he did what he always did and walked over to the couch and sat down.

It was his spot, where he sat. Mary's spot was just to the side of his own. He hadn't sat there a single time since Mary had passed, and he wouldn't ever. Nobody would. Even when everyone came over for the wake and there was nowhere else to sit, he did not allow anyone to use Mary's spot. Even, he remembered, when that little Tommy kid sat down there on accident. Everyone thought he was overreacting when he blew up on the kid and made him get up. He could easily recall the way everyone stared at him, as if he were crazy, as if he was somehow going too far. As if someone sitting in Mary's spot was no big deal at all.

That's how everyone was, though. They all wanted him to forget, to move on. It had been a few months now, and apparently that was plenty. That was just enough time to forget a living, breathing human existed. A caring one. One that loved him when no one else found him lovable. His anchor.

That's why everyone at work looked at him funny. He was the guy that just wouldn't move the hell on. The guy that moped around the office like a zombie. That was why his friends didn't call anymore as well. They didn't want to hear him drone on depressingly about how pointless life was without Mary. They didn't want him to inconvenience them with his sadness.

Except Charlie and Scott. They didn't care. They didn't mind how long Hank went on about Mary. They were real friends. Hank looked down at his phone. The two of them wouldn't be over there for a few hours still. They were coming over after he got off work, but he left work early, so he would be stuck waiting for a while. He supposed he could call them and get them over there sooner, but he figured they were probably busy with their own things. It was probably best to stick to the scheduled time.

He reached to the side of the couch and grabbed the bottle of brandy. Twisting the cap, he tilted his head back and poured a long gulp of the sweet, burning liquid down his throat. It seared on its way down.

Delicious.

He set the bottle on the table, just to the side of one of the coasters, and laid down. If he had to wait a few hours, then he would do it by sleeping. It was what he spent most of his free time doing those days anyway. Each minute sleeping was one less minute awake.

"Wake up!"

Hank shot up from the couch, his eyes darting, ready to throw fists. Until he saw that it was just Scott and Charlie. His shoulders relaxed.

"Sorry," Scott said. "You didn't answer when we knocked, so we let ourselves in."

"We're taking a lot of brandy-naps lately, I see." Charlie laughed.

"We?" Hank asked. "Why are you?"

"Same reason you are."

Hank was about to ask what that was even supposed to mean when Scott cut in. "You said you had something exciting to tell us?"

Hank nodded, trying to shake away the mild headache that lurked in the back of his skull, threatening to become a migraine. "Yeah," he said. "I did."

Hank sat back down on the couch. The night before, he had been scrolling through old text message exchanges between him and Mary when he stumbled across something. He grabbed the bottle of brandy and tucked it back away on the side of the couch in its half-assed hiding place. His sister had a new habit of stopping by unannounced to try and cheer him up, and he always noticed the mild judgement in her eyes when she saw a can of beer or liquor sitting on the table.

"I was looking through some messages between Mary and me," Hank said.

Scott nodded. Charlie just looked at him.

"We were planning, or at least planning to plan, a mountain-hiking trip in the Adirondacks. It never progressed past an idea, though."

"And you wanna do it?" Scott asked.

Hank nodded his head. "I think it's exactly what I need to clear my head. I need some nature. Some solitude. And I know it would mean a lot to Mary if I did it."

"Shit, let's do it then!" Charlie said.

Hank smiled. He was happy. He knew the two of them would be on board, or was at least pretty sure, and it was a relief to know he was right. He didn't really want to make the trip alone. He had literally no experience in mountain climbing and had watched too many movies about people getting lost in the woods.

"So, when did you want to go?" Scott asked.

Hank shrugged. "As soon as possible, I guess. I was already looking into some of the mountains last night. The Adirondacks are only a handful of hours away. There's this one called 'Snowy Mountain. It's supposed to be the tallest on the western side. There are three portions, I think. The western part, eastern, and an area called the Upper Mohawk Valley. But we're going to do Snowy Mountain because it's rated as an easier climb on all the websites."

Scott smiled. "Sounds like a plan to me."

There was a knock at the door. For the briefest of moments, Hank thought it may have been his boss from work come to ask him to come back. But that was stupid. It was his sister. It was always his sister.

He stood and walked by Scott toward the front door. Through the peephole, he saw that it wasn't his sister, nor was it his boss. It was his mother. He groaned as he pulled the door open.

He feigned a smile. "What's up, Mom?"

She didn't wait for him to invite her inside, stepping past him and forcing him to move. She nearly gagged, fanning her hand in front of her nose as she took in the house's interior.

"This place smells, Hank."

"Mom, what are you doing here?"

"Am I not allowed to stop by and see how my grieving son is doing?"

He wanted to say no. She and Mary hardly got along for reasons that Hank was still not able to fully grasp. So that led to his mother barely ever coming over, and when she did, it usually had been when Mary wasn't home. But to his surprise, even she cried at Mary's funeral. His mother never confided in him as to why she had cried, but he thought he understood on some level. Unspoken words. Stupid bad blood never put to rest. And then it was too late.

"Your sister told me the last time she had stopped here, you told her you were planning to go on some mountain-hiking trip." His mom fixed him with a quizzical look. "She said she offered to go, but you told her no?"

He didn't remember telling his sister anything about the plans, but he must have, or his mother wouldn't have been there.

"Yes. I'm going to the Adirondacks. It's something I need to do."

"It's something you need to do," she said, quietly with scorn. "What you need to do is get yourself together and give this house a good cleaning. Not go climb some mountains by yourself because you feel like you need to."

"I do need it. I need to clear my head. I need to get away from this place. And I won't be going alone." He signaled toward Scott and Charlie, who were on either side of him now. "These two are going with me."

They smiled at his mother but didn't say anything. He didn't blame them. He wouldn't want to get involved either. His mother looked at them, first Charlie, then Scott. Her face had a cringe to it, a look of disapproval, like he was trying to sell her a broken-down car.

"I don't like it," she said, much softer now. "I don't like this idea at all. I think you should stay here where your sister and I can keep an eye on you. I think you should go see that specialist your sister mentioned. Doctor Hendricks, or whatever his name was."

Hank nearly laughed out loud. *Specialist*. That's what his sister and mother insisted on calling the therapist as to not upset him. They acted like he was crazy, but both were too afraid to actually say it.

"We just don't want you being stupid. Sad people do stupid things," she said. "We're just worried."

He understood then, almost laughing as he did so. They thought he was going to go up into the mountains and kill himself, that some hikers would come along a week or so later and find him dangling from some low-hanging branch out in the middle of nowhere. They were afraid that they would have to bury a second person.

But it wasn't about them. It was about him and what he needed to do to move past this. And if while he was there, he decided to end it all, then so be it. That was his decision to make, not hers.

He walked past her, over to the door, and politely, but sternly, asked his mother to leave. She walked to the door but stopped in the opening, her truck parked along the road in the background, and looked past him one last time.

"Please stop drinking so much," she said.

He smiled wanly and told her he was going to be fine. She sighed, then asked him to consider what she had said and to just think about giving Hendricks a visit or even just a call. Just to get her to leave, he said that he would. But he wouldn't, not now and not later. He had things to do. He had a trip to plan.

Chapter 2

Hank nodded at the lady behind the counter as he entered the store. She looked at him but didn't offer a greeting back before returning to the magazine, or whatever it was, she had been looking at on the counter. Ignoring her rudeness, he proceeded over to one of the nearest aisles, the one with the jackets, boots, and backpacks for snowboarding, hiking, and other outdoor activities.

    It was his first time ever entering this store despite that fact that it was only a few blocks away from his house. Looking up and down the aisle, he realized, fully, just how little he knew about the adventure he was preparing to embark upon. He had almost no idea what he was looking for. He stared ahead at a couple of hiking backpacks hung up on a rack, unsure of how they were different from each other.

"Well, they definitely have more pockets than your average high school backpack," Scott said.

Hank waved for the counter lady to come help him. Once again, she did little to acknowledge him. Instead, she just kept talking to another woman who had joined her by the counter.

"Rude bitch," Charlie muttered. "She's probably one of those women who complains about being bored because they never have enough customers and then complains again when they have too much work to do."

"Exactly the type." Hank laughed.

A young woman carrying two ski poles under her arm looked in Hank's direction as she walked by, her eyes looking to both of Hank's sides as if she were attempting to look at the backpacks but didn't want to stop.

"I think she digs you." Charlie winked.

"She looked more confused than anything." Hank laughed. "Maybe she doesn't understand these backpacks either."

She looked back again but quickly snapped her head forward when she saw that he was looking at her as well. Maybe Charlie was right, he thought. Maybe she was checking him out. But he doubted it. She just didn't have that look in her eye, that twinkle of interest, or even a smile for that matter. If she were checking him out, she probably would have been smiling. No, it was something else. Disgust maybe? He examined himself up and down, wondering how untidy he looked, and then wondered if his breath mirrored the vast quantities of alcohol he had been consuming recently.

She was pretty, too. But he was sure, beyond a doubt, that she was not checking him out. Rather, she was looking at him like he was an insect, one that landed on the food she had just made and now had to throw out because of his contamination.

"Can I help you, sir?" The counter lady's monotonous voice startled him from his thoughts.

"Uhm...yes. Yes, you can. I'm looking for stuff for my hiking trip. Thought that these two idiots could help me, but they're about as clueless as I am." He laughed but stopped when he noticed she was not joining in.

The lady continued staring at Hank with lips so stern, so straight and unsmiling, that they could have been drawn on her face with a pencil and a ruler.

"Okay, well, do you have the money to pay for the things you're looking for?"

"The fuck kind of question is that?" Charlie snapped.

"Dude! What the hell?" Hank raised his voice. "Chill. There's no need to be like that."

He waited for the girl to snap something back, but she remained silent instead, staring at Hank not with anger but with...the same look the passing girl had given him.

"I'm sorry," he continued. "Ignore him. He's just being an ass. Please, help me find what I need."

At first, she said nothing. He thought that maybe she would throw them out. He supposed he wouldn't blame her. If someone had just yelled at him that way, he would probably want them to leave as well. If she kicked him out, though, he wasn't sure where in the hell else he could go to get these things he needed.

"Okay," she said, bringing on a wave of relief to Hank. "Follow me then."

Ten minutes later, Hank was out of the store, lugging the things he bought to the car.

"You guys could've helped a bit!" he groaned as he hoisted the backpack full of equipment into the trunk.

"A little physical exercise won't kill you." Scott grinned. "Gotta get ready for the hiking trip anyway, Hank."

By then, Hank had earned himself a terrible thirst that only a drink with an alcohol percentage of at least 40 percent could cure. Oscar's shop was close by, so he could stop there on his way home.

"Anything else you'll be needing?" Scott asked.

"Yeah. Booze," Hank answered as he pulled into a parking lot.

His was the only car there. The lot was desolate and eerily silent. At opposite ends, lone streetlamps stood high, their lights dirty and dim. Insects swarmed around the beacons like lost ships at sea. This was how Oscar's shop was every time he came by, and Hank wondered how it was still in business if this was the case.

As he got out and started across the parking lot, he suddenly felt alone out there. Alone everywhere, really. A sudden thankfulness washed over him for Charlie and Scott. They had really been there for him since Mary died. They stood by, neither of them judging him for his grieving or his alcohol problem, neither of them berating him about how he needed to move on or how he needed help. That's what real friends were for, though, he supposed.

A wave of cool, air-conditioned air hit Hank as he walked through the front doors. The place was literally buzzing with life. The various refrigerators hummed in unison, their cooling systems functioning to keep the drinks icy. The shelves were lined with clear, brilliant glass bottles. The overtop lights reflected off the bottles, making them glitter, and Hank wondered if that was intentional. It gave everything a sort of heavenly hue, like everything was sparkling.

"Hey, Hank!" Oscar shouted from across the way.

He came around the counter and started toward Hank, who had only made it a few feet into the shop so far.

"Hey, Oscar. Busy day?" Hank asked as he started perusing a shelf lined with brown bottles.

"Ain't it obvious?" Oscar grinned, gesturing to the empty store.

Hank looked up and smiled back before turning to the shelf filled with an array of liquor. He scratched his chin with a perplexed glare, wondering what drink he should go with this time. There were honestly so many options. It was like a library but for drinks.

"Lookin' for something specific?" Oscar's voice came from behind as he approached Hank.

Hank rotated a bottle and looked at the info on the back. "Something fancy for tonight. Then, something…" He paused, searching for the right word. "Something lasting for the weekend. I'm going hiking. I'd hate to do that with a clear mind." He laughed.

Oscar didn't smile at the last part of the statement. "Ain't that so? Well, good for you, Hank. Good for you. It's nice to see you…being active. So, something fancy, you said. Let me see if I can find something special for my favorite customer."

Hank looked up, unsure if he liked Oscar's compliment. Being the favorite customer at a liquor store was like…being the favorite customer at a liquor store. He tossed the comment aside and turned to watch Oscar as he started up and down some aisles.

Oscar hummed to himself; a melody Hank recognized but could not identify. Oscar looked deep in thought. Picking the perfect drink for a customer must be like an art to a guy like him. If you were going to own a shop of your own, he supposed you would have to know just about everything there was to know about what you were selling.

Oscar stopped. "Now, exactly how fancy are we talking?"

Now that he was thinking about it, Hank had never bothered with much of anything outside of brandy, rum, and whatever else could get him wasted out of his mind the quickest. All that mattered was forgetting, not what got him there.

"Fancy," Hank smiled. "Like a king."

"Well, if that's the case." Oscar turned around and headed back around the counter where a single shelf stood, bottles lining it from top to bottom. Each had its own space apart from the others, as if they were all special in some way.

"How about this?" He took down a bottle and held it up. The bottle's upper portion was fashioned into the shape of a nude woman. "Smoothest vodka around. Award winning 'n' shit."

Hank squinted his eyes, reading the gold lettering on the front. "Vroom? It's called Vroom? Like a car or…?"

"No. Don't be dumb." The man sounded outright offended. "It's Vavoom, not Vroom. And this is top-quality vodka. Way better than that shit you usually drink. And it's gluten free." He laughed at his own comment.

"Okay. Well, how much is it?"

"One hundred seventy dollars a bottle."

"Wow!"

"For fine vodka, you pay a fine price. You wanna be a king? Well, here you have it. This is a king's drink, my friend."

Hank nodded. "Okay, then. I'm sold. I'll take it."

He deserved something nice, he thought. Life had been hell, and drinking wasn't a solution, he knew that. But it was a temporary Band-Aid. A delicious, mind-numbing Band-Aid. He grabbed a couple bottles of brandy for later and met Oscar at the counter.

"So, about that hikin' trip," Oscar asked as he rang up the bottles and packed them into a paper bag and then the Vavoom into its own bag. "Tell me a little about it. You already got everythin' you need? Flasks for water, bear mace, boots?"

Hank pulled out his debit card and stuck it into the reader.

"Um, yeah, most of it. I even got this little straw that lets you drink water from creeks and stuff."

Oscar threw his head back and guffawed heartily. "Ha ha! Well, good thing you got your priorities set straight then."

He pushed the bags over to Hank, then leaned over the counter, the grin all but gone from his face, and spoke quietly, almost secretively. "By the way, where you goin' hikin' at?"

Hank put away his wallet and then situated the bags under his arm so he wouldn't drop them. "The Adirondacks."

"Damn. Way out there? You goin' alone or you got someone comin' with you?"

Hank shook his head. "No. Of course not. I wouldn't go alone. I'm not an idiot." Hank laughed. "Scott and Charlie are coming with me. I have trouble finding my way around my own block, let alone a mountain."

"Scott and Charlie?"

"Yeah, they're…" Hank turned around to see nobody there. He had just now noticed that his two friends had stayed in the vehicle. "They're waiting in the vehicle," Hank said.

Oscar squinted at the glass door, trying to peer through it, but the car was out of clear view at the edge of the lot. He seemed to retain a confused look as he diverted his gaze back up at Hank.

Hank wondered if Oscar needed glasses the way he was squinting. Oscar locked eyes with Hank and nodded briskly.

"Not sure I've met them," Oscar said. "They cool?"

"Thanks, Oscar, and yeah, you probably wouldn't have, but they're all right," Hank said before turning around to leave.

"Hank?"

Hank turned back around with raised eyebrows. He saw Oscar still leaning on the counter, but there was no trace of his perky, joking mood. Instead, Hank noticed what he thought to be concern in Oscar's eyes.

"Yeah?"

"People disappear out there, Hank. They disappear, and nobody ever finds them. And when they do turn up, they turn up dead. Not all of them. Some get found days later and become a hero in the news. But a lot of them don't. A lot of them disappear and stay gone. You be careful out there, friend."

Chapter 3

Hank closed the front door behind him, pausing in the entryway, his mind still lost in Oscar's words. People had disappeared in those mountains. Oscar wasn't wrong, and neither was his mother. He had very little climbing experience other than hiking in some local state parks. But that would pale in comparison to the Adirondacks.

His eyes tracked down the laptop sitting atop the end table by the couch, the one right next to where his drink was tucked away. A cup still rested on the table from earlier that day. He found his place on the couch, poured himself a glass of Vavoom, set it right next to the other cup, then eagerly snatched up the computer. His curiosity was beyond piqued. He had to know more. As he waited for the computer to turn on, he lifted the cup and poured a long gulp down his throat. It went down a little hot but was smooth, so smooth, just as Oscar had said it would be.

He opened a search engine and stared at the blinking vertical line as it sat awaiting his words. *Missing people in the Adirondacks.* He clicked enter. Results popped up across his screen. His eyes widened in pure awe. Tons of people had gone missing in the mountains throughout the years. Most were found, whether dead or alive. But some…some were never found at all.

He followed one of the links. It brought him to an article about a thirty-eight-year-old postal worker named David Boomhower who had gone hiking, alone, shortly after going through a divorce. The man had hoped to hike the trail that led from Northville to Lake Placid.

He didn't make it.

His body was found face-down, partially submerged in a creek, about thirty-five miles north of a small town called Gloversville. Along with his body, a diary was discovered in which the climber chronicled his sad departure into sickness and his continued hopes that he would be found. A streak of sadness ran through Hank, and he closed out the article. He wasn't sure what he had been hoping to find, maybe ghost stories or something. He had wanted to get spooked. But this…this was just sad. He felt almost as though he had caught a glimpse of something dirty, something inappropriate that he wasn't supposed to see.

He closed the laptop and set it next to him on the couch, then jumped up as if the computer was some sort of squirming, digital insect he had to get away from. He stared down at it, solitary on the cushions, imagining the secrets it held. Somewhere in the recesses of his mind, he was sickened by the morbid curiosity he felt crawling its way forward, the insatiable urge… no, the need to reopen the computer and bathe himself in the stories of the lost.

He dove back onto the couch, sweeping the laptop up in one quick motion as if it could dodge him if he were too slow. He tapped a key, and the screen came back to life, bringing forth the same article he had been reading before, a bookmark into the end of David Boomhower's life.

He clicked the back button, returning him to the results page where endless articles seemed to consume the screen. He clicked on one without even reading the headline, antsy and suddenly excited. He wished Scott and Charlie were there to read some of this with him. They would be just as excited. But they weren't. He had dropped them off at their homes, he thought, on his own way back home. But he could hardly remember it. He supposed that was one of the consequences of his drinking. He knew even then that he was digging himself deeper into the pit with each sip. But he didn't care, not anymore.

The click landed him on a page where, in the center, was an old image of a young man with long, wavy hair and a stern expression. Under the picture read *Steven Paul Thomas – circa 1976.* Hank started reading, his eyes darting across the words as he absorbed the story.

In April of 1976, a nineteen-year-old boy named Steven Paul Thomas was invited by his friend Bruce Weaver to join him and five other college students on a hike to the top of Mount Marcy, the tallest of the Adirondack peaks. The mountains were dangerous at that time of the year, all of them, but especially Mount Marcy with its large, expansive landscape and towering peak. Take one wrong turn and you could end up lost. Take two wrong turns and you were dead.

To one side of the mountain was a particularly secluded area called Panther Gorge, a section of forest tucked away between Mount Marcy and Mount Haystack. It was filled with streams and incredibly dense brush, an abyss within an abyss. He shivered at the thought and immediately marked Marcy off his mental list of mountains he may climb.

It was reported that Steven didn't get along well with many of the group's members and remained very quiet the entire climb up. This immediately intrigued Hank. Why would he go on a trip to such a place with people he didn't even like? And could it have been murder?

He read on.

At that time of the year, the mountain was still covered in snow. Up high, temperatures easily reached frozen lows, threatening exposure and hypothermia. To make the adventure more interesting, Steven had brought marijuana. They stopped at around three thirty p.m. at the lower plateau lean-to called Hopkins. Despite being only a mile or so away from the peak, the group thought it best to make for the summit in the morning with it being so bitterly cold and wet out that day.

But Steve didn't want to wait. Despite his friend's protests, Steve decided he wanted to scout out the area ahead and left the camp in nothing but a t-shirt, boots, jeans, and a yellow rain slicker—no map, no compass, and, Hank thought...*no hope.*

He never came back.

The search for Steven Paul Thomas involved rangers, volunteers, and helicopters. Steve's brother, Bob, climbed the mountain over six hundred times in search of his little brother. But Steven was never found, living or dead.

Hank no longer thought it had been murder. Instead, to him, it sounded like a classic case of stupidity and bad decision making. What could drive someone to leave their camp alone in freezing temperatures? Overconfidence, he assumed. Or maybe the others were being assholes and he just wanted to get away. Maybe he wanted to reach the summit and experience the success for himself, without the taint of those he didn't like surrounding him. Whatever the case was, the kid was dead now, and only the stories of the survivors would ever be told, and Hank knew well that these stories would likely never be the full truth. It was the same way with everything else in history. History was told by the winners, those that lived, however they chose to tell it.

With a deep breath, he returned back to the search screen. He felt now like he had already been on an adventure of his own, living the sad life of those lost in the mountains. With only a scroll of his mouse, the names kept flowing. Jack Coloney. George Woltjen, a sixty-year-old hunter from Queens. George LaForest, a fisherman from Stillwater. Irene Horne, a wanderer and hitchhiker. Thomas Messick, an eighty-two-year-old who vanished while hunting. The list went on and on.

One such case that caught Hank's eye and held it for a minute was that of Douglas Legg, an eight-year-old who went missing in 1971. He had been preparing to hike with family near their seasonal home in the Santanoni Preserve by Newcomb, New York. He was asked by his uncle to walk the very short distance back to the house to change into some longer pants to avoid the poison ivy which lined the trails.

Over six hundred people helped in the search for Douglas. Some say the number was actually in the thousands. Helicopters flew overhead. It was the largest search ever done at the time. But, just like with Steven Paul Thomas, no trace of him was ever found.

He scrolled away from the article, not wanting to read more. He wondered what in the world the uncle had been thinking letting the boy go back alone but then remembered how different parenting had been back then. Even when Hank was little, in the early nineties, parenting was vastly different then than it was in 2021. Back then, at the age of eight, he remembered hopping on his bicycle and riding off for hours with nothing but a portable CD player and a couple of buddies. Now, if he had a kid, if Mary had lived longer and they had had a baby of their own, he couldn't begin to imagine letting his little one ride off alone with nothing—not even a cell phone—,and disappearing, for hours at a time. Even if he were older, like eleven or twelve, he wasn't sure he would allow it.

Part of him wanted to close the laptop, to allow the stories to rest along with those that were never found. But so many of the stories; Douglas Legg, David Boomhower, Steven Paul Thomas, all of them were from so long ago, the seventies and nineties. He wondered, with all the advances in technology and tracking they now had, if people still disappeared. He thought about the modern age, how you could track the exact location of a person just because they had a phone in their pocket, if the movies were true, that is, and wondered how in a world with a constantly exploding population, someone could just…vanish.

The excitement he had felt maybe a half hour earlier had dwindled into something far less alive, something morbid and sad. He wanted to go on, to read further, but not because he truly wanted to, not for fun or for pleasure, at least, but because he had to. It was from an instinctual, deep-seeded curiosity. Something ancient, something that Hank thought lived somewhere within all people. The curiosity that killed the cat, he thought to himself. Maybe if he read more, some of the information could help him not to make the same mistakes all these other people had made.

After taking another quick drink, which he had been doing throughout the time reading the articles, he placed his fingers back on the keys and considered what to search for. His vision had begun to shift around, vertigo finally setting in from the drinks even though he was sitting in place. *Adirondack Mountains new disappearances*, he typed. Results came up. But strangely, none of them were very new at all. He guessed that was kind of what he was hoping for. After all, he didn't really want to get lost out there. What he was searching for was reassurance, something to tell him that these disappearances were a thing of the past.

Then he came across an article that looked particularly interesting about a skier disappearing from a mountain called Whiteface. Even the mountain's name, he thought, sounded a little intimidating. He didn't even know people skied on those mountains. He was under the impression that they were covered from head-to-toe in forest.

The article was about a man named Constantinos "Danny" Filippidis. As he skimmed the first few lines, Hank's eyes opened wide with awe. This man hadn't simply disappeared. He kept skimming, now even faster, thinking he would for sure find something suggesting that this whole article was some sort of joke. But he didn't. It was true. Danny Filippidis, a man from Toronto, Canada, according to the article, disappeared from Whiteface Mountain in eastern New York and was found six days later, dazed and confused, in Sacramento, California, still wearing his skiing gear.

Once the man was oriented enough to give a statement, he told the police that all he remembered was being picked up by a truck, getting dropped off in California, buying a cell phone, and getting a haircut. He didn't know why he could remember nothing else. He did remember sleeping, though, lots and lots of sleeping.

Hank's first thought was that maybe this guy had been picked up by some sort of gang he owed money to or something. But why would he have been taken to California? And from the little he knew, he didn't appear to be harmed in any way. He scanned the article for mention of drugs but saw nothing of the sort.

They spent nearly ten thousand searching hours, over the course of six days, on finding this guy, and somehow, magically, he appeared across the country. *Magically*. That was a word that seemed to fit perfectly. But he didn't believe in magic. He didn't believe in a lot of things. But when all the natural explanations seemed illogical, did that leave only the supernatural to fill the void?

Hank's phone rang. It startled him from his thoughts. Darkness circled all around him. Night had fallen while he was lost in the stories. Only a single beacon lit the otherwise black interior, and that was the clock light on the stove across the way in the kitchen.

He pulled his phone out and saw that it was his mother calling. He closed the laptop and put the phone to his ear, answering with a feigned tiredness.

"Yeah, Mom?"

The line remained silent for a few long seconds before his mother finally spoke.

"Honey, I'm really not sure you should be going out to some mountains. It's dangerous. You could get lost. I don't think you should go."

Hank smiled, happy now, with seeing all the heartbreak in those articles, that his mother was concerned. "It's fine, Mom. It's not like I'll be alone. I'll be with Scott and Charlie."

"I'm not so sure I like that either," his mom said. "You've been acting strange. And then this Scott and this Charlie show up? I don't even remember you mentioning these two before. How do you know them? How do you know you can trust them to keep you safe all the way out there?"

"Fine," he said, not wanting to argue with his mother any longer. "I won't go. You're right."

"You won't?"

Of course he would go. He had to. For the first time in the months since his wife passed, he had thought about something other than her, and her smile, and her love. He hadn't forgotten about her. That was impossible. But he had thought about something other than his pain. He had a goal now. These mountains, they intrigued him. He had to go. He had to experience them for himself.

He smiled, staring off into the darkness, toward the dim light that shined from the stove. "No, Mom. I won't go."

"Good. Now come over tomorrow and I'll fix you one of your favorite dishes."

"Sure, Mom."

"You can bring your friends, too, if you want. I think I should get to know them better."

Hank grinned even bigger, intrigued with the idea but doubtful Scott and Charlie would be too interested in the idea. It seemed juvenile, and they were adults. But he didn't want to sour the conversation by telling her no.

"Maybe. I've got to go, Mom. I'm pretty tired. Talk to you soon?"

"Okay." There was a brief pause. "I love you, honey."

"Love you too, Mom," he said, then pushed the end call button, bringing the conversation to a close and the room to darkness.

Chapter

4

He could feel the square-shaped lump in his dress pants pocket, its contents a weight that had been weighing on his mind. His heart rocked within his chest, heavier than it had in years, even heavier than it had the first time he laid eyes on her at the office Christmas party. If she didn't get there soon, he was worried his heart may just give out and just stop right there, leaving him for her to find, dead on the floor.

    That may be the easier option, he thought, laughing faintly to himself. But just then, a girl dressed in a skin-tight, knee-length black dress entered the rooftop, greeted at the door by a well-dressed host. The man signaled for her to follow and guided her to where Hank sat nervously at a small circular table. He pulled the chair out for her, and she sat, the beautiful smile he loved shining brightly along her cheeks.

"Thank you," she said in a near whisper as the man placed menus in front of them.

Once the host was gone, she took a moment to look around shamelessly, her eyes wide with astonishment. He had never taken her somewhere this nice. Quite frankly, it was out of his budget, but for the occasion, he needed the location to be some place she would never forget. Beams connected above them, gleaming light fixtures dangling from them, spaced out so seamlessly that they almost looked like stars at a glance. Beyond them were the real stars, speckling the night sky, lighting the rooftop of the world.

"This place is really nice," she said.

But he barely heard her. He couldn't take his eyes off of her eyes, her lips, her…everything. She glowed like a princess atop her throne. Her eyes pulled at him like an endless siren song, like her gaze was where he truly belonged, where he lived, and where he was meant to be until the end of time.

"Babe."

He snapped out of it and smiled.

"Yeah?"

"Can we afford this place?"

His smile nearly faded. He couldn't, but that didn't matter. "Yes. We can afford it, this one time at least."

He tried to laugh playfully. They had been budgeting for quite some time, ever since they left the company they had worked at and met. It was technically against the rules to date within the company, and even worse, it turned out that their boss, whom Mary worked directly under as an assistant, had some sort of crush on her. So, when she and Hank started dating, he started acting differently, difficult toward her, criticizing most everything she did. She had considered reporting him to human resources but, as they both knew, dating within the company was against the rules anyway.

So, they quit. They found new jobs. Hers, just as before, was better. Her business degree gave her a bit of a leg-up. But the company where he started working provided a lot of room to grow, ample opportunities to move up the corporate ladder. Once that happened, they could afford to eat at places like this whenever they wanted.

"It's beautiful," she said, looking off into the distance at all the tall buildings that lined the horizon.

She noticed out of the corner of her eye that he was staring at her, not at the starry sky or the buildings like she had been. Her cheeks flushed red, and she turned back to him.

"You're staring."

He smiled. "I can't help it. You're just so beautiful." He paused; their eyes locked. "From the moment I first saw you—"

"At the Christmas party?" She laughed.

He nodded. "From the moment I first saw you at the Christmas party, I knew I wanted to be here with you some day, in this moment."

The waiter walked up, awkwardly interrupting his poorly planned speech. "Are you ready to order?"

Hank just looked at him, unsure for a moment if he wanted to strangle the guy or order food. But if he tried to eat now, he wasn't sure he could stop himself from being sick with nerves. This was his chance, his out; just like when he stood outside the party, this interruption was his opportunity to run away. He shook his head no. But he didn't want to. Never before had he wanted so badly to be where he was. He had to ask now, and if he ordered, and the food got there after she had turned his proposal down, he wouldn't be able to eat. Even though he didn't think she would say no, he couldn't help but consider the possibility and the wasted food and the bill he would amass before leaving in tears.

The waiter finally noticed Hank's silence and walked away, leaving them to continue. "Anyway," he fake-laughed. "As I was saying…"

That's when he noticed the tears that were already filling her eyes. He frowned. "Are you okay?"

"No," she said. "I mean, yes. Yes. I'm fine. I'm great. Please go on."

"Oh-okay." He fidgeted and then reached for his pocket, trying to pull the square box out without her seeing, but his heart was skipping out of control because he was pretty sure she had caught on to what was happening. "I knew from the beginning that I wanted to be with you here someday. I knew, I think, even then, and now—"

He stood, stepped around the side of the table, and then lowered down to one knee. "That I wanted to spend the rest of my life with you. I can't imagine a life any other way. I don't want to imagine my life any other way. I just want to be with you now, and forever."

Her eyes finally broke, the dam collapsing as tears began rolling down her cheeks, smearing the bit of makeup she had on. She was nearly shaking.

He looked up at her, from down on his knee, her smile weak and her eyes glimmering with happiness, and asked her the question he had waited so long to ask. "Mary Hawkins, will you marry me?"

Hank woke the next morning feeling down about having lied to his mother. But that didn't matter now because it couldn't. He had to move on, to keep focus on the journey ahead. And boy was it going to be just that. Before they left town, though, there was one thing he needed to do, something he had been putting off for a while, afraid of what dread and sorrow it could wrench up from deep inside him.

Placing his feet over the side of the bed, Hank stood and stretched so hard he was mildly surprised his arms didn't pop right out of their sockets. The sudden stench of body odor rushed into his nostrils, and he cringed. As if to make sure the odor didn't somehow belong to someone else, he tilted his head downward and took a quick sniff of his pit.

He nearly gagged. Oh, it was him, that much was for sure. He wondered now how long it had been since he had showered and then wondered how nobody else had noticed his smell or why they hadn't told him. Maybe this was how a sorry-sack was supposed to smell. Now that he was thinking about it, he couldn't really recall the last time he had showered. Most everything in his life was one big blur those days. Before he left, he would need to clean himself.

After his shower, Hank found himself standing in front of the mirror, taking in the mess he had become for the first time in weeks. The area around his eyes was tinted blue and sunken in, sort of resembling a poorly-put-together Halloween costume or a dead person. He picked up his comb, wet it in the sink, and combed his hair off to one side.

"So, we ready to go?" Charlie said, barging into the bathroom.

Hank jumped, startled by the entrance. "Dude!" he yelled, thankful he had already put on his boxers. "Get out of here, ya weirdo. I'm not even dressed yet."

As Hank exited the bathroom, he noticed Scott giving him a strange stare, so he returned it.

Scott smiled. "Nice hair. There must be a special occasion."

Hank just lifted his brow, almost wanting to tell his friend to mind his own business.

Scott continued. "I think I know what the occasion might be. It's been a long time. You visiting her today?"

Hank shuffled through the drawers, throwing clothes on as he found them. He didn't answer, though, by the way Scott was looking at him, he didn't need to. Sometimes it was like Scott could read his damn mind. Both of them, really.

Charlie laughed. "He must be. A shower *and* nice hair. He's even putting on clean clothes for a change."

"You two going to just stand around watching me get dressed and asking stupid questions? Fricken idiots."

Charlie held his chest, then stumbled back as he spoke. "Oh, Hank, you're always stabbing me in the heart with your words."

"You don't have a heart," Scott said.

Hank laughed, his mind momentarily pulling away from his wife and the question of what he was going to say to her once he was finally face to face with her again.

"Let's get going," Hank said. "We have a lot to do."

Fully dressed, Hank made his way back into the bathroom. In the mirror, he saw a version of himself that he hadn't laid eyes on since before everything. He looked…good, he thought. It was a version of himself that he could get used to seeing again. He wasn't sure what this feeling was. Hope, maybe? Unable to help it, he smiled, then headed off to pack.

He lugged the equipment to the car trunk and set it in with a light thud. His backpack was heavy with all the things they had picked up for the trip. He took in a deep breath, his body's quick descent into exhaustion reminding him of how out of shape he really was. He guessed that was what sitting around and moping for months did to a person.

Charlie and Scott stood alongside the vehicle watching him sweat. "Thanks for all the help," Hank said sarcastically.

Charlie laughed. "Don't mention it."

Scott only nodded.

Hank stepped back, closing the trunk before rounding the side toward the front of the car.

"You know what else we should pick up? A tent," Charlie said. "In case we decide we want to camp up there or something."

Scott had the door open and was about to get in. "That's a pretty good idea." Scott seemed to suddenly have a gleam in his eye. "We could set it up at the top of the mountain and look at the stars. It would really clear the head."

Charlie shrugged. "A little corny, but he does have a point."

"I don't know, guys. Camping at the top of a mountain?" He considered it for a minute. He wasn't sure if it was a good idea, and it would probably be rough trying to carry a tent up a mountain. But he had been holding himself down far too often since Mary left him, and this trip was supposed to be all about change. "You know what? Screw it. Let's do it."

Hank got in the car. Charlie and Scott followed. They drove back in the direction of the outdoors store, but Hank cranked the wheel early, pulling them into the parking lot of a small strip mall.

"What are we doing here?" Charlie asked.

His question was answered when Hank pulled the car up in front of a flower shop called *Lilly's Blossoms*. He got out without a word and headed inside. A wall of fragrance collided with him the moment he walked through the doors. He was glad then that he didn't suffer from allergies, or he would probably be on the ground convulsing.

He knew exactly what he was looking for, just not what they looked like. He perused the aisles for just a minute before a very pretty woman approached him with a bright smile and a greeting.

"Is there anything I can help you find?"

For just a split second, Hank felt guilty for taking in the girl's stunning beauty so willingly. She had long red hair and just a light sprinkle of freckles lining her cheeks.

"Ummm, yes." He composed himself. "Yes. I'm looking for cherry blossoms. My wife, she used to have this garden when she was little, and she loved the cherry blossoms. But I don't know what those look like. She's—she's not with us anymore. I wanted to get them for her grave. I'm on my way to visit her now."

He realized he was rambling and stopped.

"I'm sorry. I—if you could show me where the cherry blossoms are, please."

Her cheeks had turned red, and she looked uncomfortable. "Absolutely, right this way."

He followed her, cursing himself inside for going on about such a sad topic. This woman was just trying to do her job, and here he was having a mental malfunction in her store.

When they came to a stop, he didn't have to be told which flowers amongst the many were his wife's cherry blossoms. They were beautiful. The petals were white, fading into a pink so effortlessly, as if the two colors were really one, and all that mattered, all that determined which it would be, was how the flower felt in that moment. In some places, the flowers were so pink, it was as if they were trying to become red but couldn't quite do it.

When Hank got back in the car, he didn't say anything. He merely handed the flowers to Scott to hold and started the car. They had to swing by the other store really quick and grab a tent before heading to the cemetery.

He found a nice five-to-eight-person tent that came with a decent, easy-to-hold carrying case, so he chose that one. Plus, it would give the three of them extra space, so that they weren't laying practically on top of one another. While there, Hank picked some other things that he had forgotten, miscellaneous items that years of watching television and some common sense told him he may need, such as a compass, an outdoor tactical knife in case he needed to cut kindling, and an emergency first-aid kit, the last of which he couldn't believe he had forgotten to get the first time around.

There were no cars parked in the small dirt parking lot of the Ashbrooke Cemetery. In the distance, he could see and hear a man moving along in a riding lawnmower near the back end. Hank pulled up, opting to walk the rest of the way even though there were narrow roads leading all throughout the cemetery.

The dirt had settled, and grass had already begun to overtake the surface of Mary's grave. But a few daffodils grew up as well, reaching high into the sky almost as if they knew he were coming with other flowers to join them and were excited. He knelt on one knee and set the bouquet of cherry blossoms next to the daffodils and whispered, "These are for you."

Charlie and Scott stood beside him. A tear escaped from the edge of Hank's eye as he thought about Mary. God, he wished she were there. He would do anything. If Mary were with him for this trip, they'd have the adventure of a lifetime. She was always up for an adventure, anytime or anyplace. From the first night he was with her, he knew, they'd be together forever. They talked about having a family, going camping with them, and fishing. He'd teach their kids about setting up a tent, and Mary would take them on hikes. But now it didn't matter; he was all alone, with only his two friends to keep him company. Forever turned out to be a lot shorter than he had expected.

He began to speak, choking on the words as they left his drying throat. "I wish you were coming with me, Babe. But…I guess—I guess you'll be sitting this one out." A weep escaped, almost turning into a sob. "But I do have these two wiseasses, I suppose. They'll have to do for now. I think you'd like them. I really do."

"So, does this mean we have her permission to go with you?" Charlie laughed.

Scott nudged Charlie with his elbow. "Cut him a break, man. The guy lost his wife."

"It's all right, Scott, I don't mind. I think maybe joking around a little might help, even if it's Charlie's shitty jokes." Hank turned his head, giving Charlie a smile.

Wiping his eyes, Hank stood, sniffled, gave one last long look at his wife's grave, and then turned back toward the car. If he stayed too long, he was afraid he may never want to leave. Plus, they had about six hours of driving ahead of them, so they really needed to get going now; they were burning daylight. As Hank got behind the wheel, he hesitated, then reached behind himself, opened the cooler, and grabbed the crystalline bottle of Vavoom. Looking to the cemetery, he opened the top, smiled, then tilted it back, and said, "This one is for you…my love."

He downed one long swig of the king's vodka, feeling it singe as it trailed down his esophagus. But he welcomed the pain. It made him feel alive. He took in a deep breath and then sealed the bottle and returned it. He felt Scott's stare on him as he closed the cooler lid. He hadn't told either of them he would be bringing alcohol. He thought he heard a light snicker from Charlie and avoided Scott's eyes altogether, turning back around to face the front.

Most of the trip was about as boring as boring could be. Both Charlie and Scott fell asleep at various points, leaving Hank jealously alone and awake. With each minute that ticked away, he had to argue with himself not to stop for the night. Three hours turned into two, and then into one. He wanted to make it there before night officially fell. He didn't want to find a place now and have to drive even further in the morning. He was sure that more driving would leave him feeling tired by the time they made it to the mountains.

Hank was in awe when the mountains started coming into view. Despite still being miles out, he could see the peaks standing overtop the sky like guardians. He wondered which one was Snowy Mountain. He couldn't be sure yet, but his anticipation was high.

"We can stop here."

Scott jerked awake, looking around as if he had temporarily forgotten where he was. Charlie yawned in the back. Both turned and looked at the glowing neon sign as they pulled into a motel parking lot.

"We're gonna stop here for the night. We need to get some sleep so we can be up and ready first thing in the morning," Hank said.

"Yeah, yeah. Sleep," Charlie said through yawns. "Sleep sounds good."

As Hank got out, the sun was moving further behind one of the peaks, shedding beams of light across the sky like the mountains were physically cutting the sun in half. The motel was a two-story structure with railings lining the upper floor. The place looked a little outdated and a bit creepy, but they were only staying there for the night, so it didn't matter. He wasn't sure what their lodging plans for the rest of their trip would be—whether they would camp the entire time or find a cozy cabin to hold out in—but that seemed like an afterthought as sleep pulled at Hank's eyes. They were taking things as they came, and he was fine with that. That's what made it an adventure.

After parking the car, Hank, leaving Charlie and Scott with the car to watch their belongings, walked up to the motel's front office. The inside looked even more outdated than the outside, and he hoped, for a moment, that there were no bedbugs or anything of that type hidden in the rooms. There were a couple chairs on one side of the lobby, with a table between them, and a television monitor on the wall, playing the latest weather report. On the opposite side sat a station with complimentary coffee and tea. But from where Hank stood, he wasn't sure he would trust either. The pot looked faded, maybe even dirty. An attendant sat behind the counter watching a ball game but turned to greet Hank when she heard the chime of the doorbell.

She smiled; her teeth were tinted yellow from the cigarettes he could smell in the air. "Hi, how can I help you?"

"Hello. Can I get a room for three, please?"

Looking at him blankly, she said, "The biggest we have is two, but there's a complimentary couch in each room that should be big enough for someone to sleep on if they had to."

"Okay. That should be fine, I guess."

She looked to Hank's sides, to the lobby sitting area, then toward the entrance, as he dug into his pocket to retrieve his wallet. "Where are your guests?"

"Oh, they're in the car waiting for me."

"Okay, well, they'll need to sign in, too." She pointed at a clipboard with a list of names on it, a pen attached to it by a small chain.

"I'll sign for them, if that's okay?"

She considered the question, then answered with a hint of annoyance. "Okay, whatever, as long as you can vouch for them if they break anything. If your name is the only one on the list, you'll have to pay for any and all damages."

"I can vouch. We're pretty boring. You won't have any problems with us." He tried to laugh, but it came out sounding just as fake and awkward as it felt.

Hank handed the lady his credit card. After she swiped it, a paper printed from behind the desk. She promptly slid it across the counter. He quickly jotted his signature and passed it back.

"You're all set. Check out's eleven a.m., no free breakfast, sorry."

"No problem, we just need a place to stay for the night, then we'll be on our way."

Leaving the office, Hank made his way to the car. Charlie was waiting outside, leaning against the trunk, looking wanly at the mountains surrounding them on almost all sides, while Scott sat inside the car, doing what, Hank wasn't sure.

When Charlie saw Hank coming, he smiled and said, "Isn't this beautiful? I can't wait to get up there and see what happens. You get the room all set?"

"Yep, only got two beds, though, and a couch. Biggest they had."

"I'm not sleeping on a couch. It'd kill my back," Charlie said.

Scott, who had gotten out of the car and was listening to the conversation, cut in. "Don't worry, I'll take it."

"Nah, it's cool," Hank said. "I'll take the couch. I've been spending half my nights at home on the couch anyway." Because sleeping in the bed alone had long since become too painful to bear.

Hank went to the trunk and opened it, retrieving a small bag of toiletries and a change of clothes, leaving the rest of the gear and his personal backpack behind.

"You got all our stuff?" Charlie called back to Hank as he started toward the motel.

Hank gave Charlie a thumbs-up but didn't follow yet. He stayed at the car for another few minutes, staring up into the orange-streaked sky, toward the mountains, as if something was there, something staring back at him amongst all that darkness.

Hank fiddled with the key, trying to get it into the old motel lock. When he did, the door opened with a little difficulty, grabbing the carpet and sticking for a second before freeing and opening all the way. The room could be described as nothing other than "economy." There were two beds, but they were so close to each other, they were practically one. He wondered what shitty, homophobic comment Charlie would make about that when he finally got in there.

There was a small loveseat-sized couch off to the right of the beds, just a few feet away from a small bedside stand. Across the room from the couch was a small flat-screen television attached the wall, the cord winding down along the wall and hanging there, no plug outlet in sight. He walked over and set his bag alongside the couch and let out a yawn of his own. There was no doubt in his mind that he would pass out cold the moment he laid down. There was a bathroom leading off the room a couple feet from the television, but he didn't care about that right then. Any teeth brushing or showering would have to wait until the morning.

He laid down and rested his head on the firm arm of the couch and covered up with a blanket that had been resting at the edge of the couch. By the time Scott and Charlie came in, Hank was already sound asleep.

Chapter

5

Mary handed him the pregnancy test, the bedroom dark aside from the bathroom light shining in through the open door. It had only one line on it, the control line. It was negative. She wasn't pregnant, still.

They had dated for years, loved each other for years, and been married for years. The next step, Hank thought, should be a baby. He had always wanted a child, an heir, someone to continue his family name. It wasn't as if his family name carried any weight, but his sister would likely take her boyfriend's last name, leaving only him to pass down the name.

But the test said negative, again. They had tested multiple times over the last few months, and each one had been negative. No matter how many times they tried, their attempts always failed. This time felt different, though, because Mary's period had been late. He felt confident that a baby in her belly was the reason why. But it wasn't.

He groaned, tossing the test into the bedside garbage, alongside Mary's tissues, then sat down next to Mary. Mary didn't say anything. He didn't blame her. It wasn't even the fact that she still wasn't pregnant that was frustrating him in that moment. What bothered him was that she didn't seem to care, at least not for the same reasons he did. He saw no emotion in her eyes when she had handed it to him, telling him as she did so that it was negative.

She would tell him that she wanted to have a kid with him. She would say it with such honesty, with such sincerity in her voice. But he had overheard her one time on the phone with her mother telling her that she didn't really want a child. He looked at the tissues in the trash. She was upset, he thought, not because she wasn't pregnant with his child, but with the fact that she was having trouble getting pregnant to begin with.

If she didn't want a kid, then he wanted her to be honest with him about it, not lie. Perhaps he was just being selfish. But if she could lie so easily, so well, about something so important to him, then what else could she be lying about? He tried to tell himself that those were crazy thoughts, that he was overreacting. But he wasn't. He had heard the words firsthand. He had heard her say them with his own ears.

He felt like a fool. Because here she was again, lying about being upset, about hoping for a positive next time as she hugged him at the bedside. She kissed him on the cheek and pulled him in close.

"I love you," she whispered.

And he loved her, too. More than the world. But for the first time ever, with the most dreadful sinking feeling infecting the pit of his stomach, he wondered if she really did love him or if that was a lie, too.

The bright mountain sun cascaded through the gaps in the curtains, beaming down into the room where it started on the floor but slowly turned along with time until the beam rested directly on Hank's shut eyes. First, he tried to swat the light away as if it were a dream or an annoying insect. But it wasn't, and minutes later, he finally sprung awake. He sat forward in a sudden jerk, the dream he had just been immersed in quickly becoming nothing more than a distant memory.

It took a moment for his eyes to adjust, but when they did, he became confused if only for a moment about where he was, or how he got there, before the fact came flooding back. He glanced out the window, seeing picturesque mountains towering over the horizon in the distance.

He was in the Adirondacks with Scott and Charlie, who were also waking up just then, both yawning and rubbing their eyes. Despite sleeping on a couch, a crappy couch for that matter, he felt surprisingly rested, which was good given the day they had ahead of them.

"Up and at 'em!" Hank said as he stood up from the couch and stretched.

Charlie groaned, and so did Scott. But, after rolling around in refusal, both eventually got up from their beds and started sluggishly getting ready. They wasted no time from there. With their bags packed, Scott and Charlie headed outside while Hank went to the front desk to check them out. He approached the desk but saw nobody, even after peeking around behind the glass as if the woman would be hiding on the floor. So, instead of waiting around, he set the room keys on the counter and gave a holler.

"Room seven is heading out!"

Scott and Charlie were standing at each side of the car laughing as Hank approached. They stopped as soon as Hank got near. He wanted to ask what was so funny but decided he didn't care.

"Get in the car," he said.

They drove for a short while, Hank trying to keep an eye on his GPS, the other two staring out the windows, marveling at the mountains around them. They stopped once in a drive-thru to grab some breakfast, not wanting to waste what little food they had brought until they were actually on the mountain. Other than that, they continued straight on through until they reached their destination, the base of Snowy Mountain.

They pulled up along the side of the road where, just across the street, there was a sign that welcomed them to Snowy Mountain. Off to the side of it was the beginning of the trail. Even from within his vehicle, Hank could see the trail snaking off into the woods, into the depths where civilization no longer held a grip, into a place from which some men never returned.

They got out and started grabbing gear from the trunk. Hank hoisted the tent up onto his back. Charlie and Scott grabbed the rest. A car whizzed by, leaving a cool breeze trailing behind, which hit Hank with a refreshing chill. It was a little cool out, but it was still pretty early in the morning.

Two long pieces of wood shaped like logs formed a "T" arch. From one end of that "T" hung a small sign which Hank read as he approached. *Trail to: Snowy Mt. Summit.* Through the "Trail to" ran a yellow arrow, starting on one side of the words and ending on the other, pointing toward where the trail began.

Hank's mouth hung wide as he read the rest of the sign aloud. "Three thousand eight hundred ninety-nine–foot elevation. Three-point-four miles to the top."

Honestly, he wasn't all that familiar with how tall other mountains were, but nearly four thousand feet—that seemed like a lot. For reference, he did the math really quick in his head and considered that that would be equal to about thirteen football fields stacked atop each other. The sign told him to follow the markers. *Don't worry, I plan to,* he thought to himself.

Charlie had already started toward the trailhead, so Hank hurried along. The path immediately started climbing. Massive, thick roots bulged up from under the ground, forming what Hank could only describe as scattered stairs. It almost felt like nature was daring him to continue, like it was welcoming him, even saying, "Here, I'll make it easy for you." The thought chilled him.

He started up the trail, his thighs immediately burning as they lifted him up the root staircase. He tried his best to ignore it. The breeze was cool against his skin under the shadowed canopy above. The air smelled like nature, perfectly, in a way no artificial scent could ever truly replicate. Insects swarmed around his head, not mosquitos, but some other breed of annoyance.

When the breeze picked up, he could hear the sounds of bushes and trees fluttering and rustling. When it got quiet, he could hear an almost absolute silence, infiltrated only by the slightest of sounds, those that you could miss if you stopped paying attention for even a second, the ones brought into existence by the life that hid among the trees and among the shrubs.

Once they passed the initial root stairs, the landscape calmed a little, turning into simple, normal trails. They followed with a gradual increase in steepness as the mountain climbed toward its peak. Hank tried to put the exhaustion out of his mind by talking to Scott and Charlie, but they didn't seem to have much to say with the trail kicking both of their asses as well.

They finally came to a stop and pulled bottles of water from their bags. Hank chugged his like someone was going to steal it from him if he didn't get it down quick enough. Looking back the way they came, he wondered exactly how far they had progressed so far. It felt like they had been going forever, but he knew that not to be true. Part of him wanted to take out his phone just to check, but he knew that if the truth was substantially less than his expectations, it would be disheartening.

Hank heard a sound. His head sprung up like a deer. The sound was becoming clearer and pulled his eyes back toward the way they had come. In the distance, just barely visible between the trees, he could see two people walking and talking.

"Let's get going, guys," Hank said.

He didn't want two others giggling at his exhaustion. He was having a rough enough time already, and they probably weren't even halfway up the mountain. Scott and Charlie started walking ahead, seeming not to notice the two people heading their way.

They continued walking, moving over and past the many obstacles on the trail, until the two following behind them evaporated from his mind. At some points, the tree-cover was so thick, the sunlight struggled to break the barrier, leaving spread-out rays of light raining down on them like a disco ball.

"There's someone up there," Scott said.

Immediately remembering the two from earlier, Hank whirled around to look back, but to his surprise, the two people were nowhere to be seen. But Scott said "up there," not behind them. He turned back around just as they were rounding a slight corner. Directly in front of them were three people, one a younger woman, the other two older—a man and a woman. They all looked at the guys as they approached.

The old woman was sitting on a tipped tree and, seeing them approaching, pulled her legs in toward herself. "I'm sorry," she said. "Let me get out of your way."

She wasn't really blocking the way to begin with. "It's okay." Hank laughed fakely. "Is everything okay?"

"Oh, yes," the older man said. "We're just a little tired. This climbing thing is a lot harder than you imagine it will be."

"You don't have to tell me," Hank said, looking down at his legs. "These things can climb stairs, but beyond that, they aren't very useful."

Everyone laughed. The couple were in their late fifties, Hank guessed. Older but apparently not too old to tackle a mountain. She was wearing jeans and a long-sleeve shirt, a necklace around her neck with a cross on it. She looked young for her age just as the man did. He wore jeans as well but had a short-sleeve shirt on with a baseball logo on the front. He had no necklace on but wore glasses and a short head of hair, nearly buzzcut. He admired them and scoffed at himself now for being so weak and out of shape. At their age, he would have a plump belly and barely be able to make it up the stairs, let alone a mountain.

"Ten years ago," the man said. "This probably would have been a cinch. I used to play basketball when I was younger. This would have been nothing."

Hank just nodded. He was more than ten years younger than the man and was having a rough time, but he wasn't going to reiterate it and embarrass himself further. The woman placed her hands on her legs and pushed herself up to her feet.

The younger woman was just standing there, smiling at everybody. Her hair was long and brown, her eyes a forest green. She wore a thin blue hoodie with a purple shirt peeking out from underneath. Around her neck, she had a fancy camera dangling, a Nikon or something, he wasn't really sure.

The older woman patted the dirt from the butt of her pants. "I suppose we should start to get going."

Just then, she looked past Hank at something behind him. It confused him at first, but then he turned around to see two other people approaching them. Despite not having seen much of the two that were following earlier, he knew right away that these must have been them. It was a man and woman, both, Hank thought, probably a little younger than him. The girl was smiling, the guy less so.

"Hello," the girl said with a wave.

Her smile was bright and welcoming. Hank suddenly found himself admiring her beauty, her long, red hair and peppered freckles. He shook away the thought before the man, he guessed her boyfriend, noticed him staring and got upset about it.

"Is everything all right? We saw you all stopped up ahead."

"Yes," the old woman said. "Yes, I'm fine. Just a bit tired. But I think I'm okay now."

"I'm not surprised," she said. "It's a tall mountain. Rough terrain. You're brave to even try it."

The old woman smiled at this, her cheeks turning a little red as she glanced over at her husband.

"We could follow you up if you want," she said. "We've done this mountain about a hundred times. We could make sure you guys get up there all right."

"Oh no," she said. "I wouldn't dream to bother. It's fine. We're actually going up with our friend Jennifer."

The girl who was with the older couple waved at the crowd but still didn't say anything, having been silent the entire time since Hank and the others showed up.

"She climbs a lot. We should be okay in her hands, I think."

"You sure? I mean..."

"They're fine," the younger man said. "They said they don't need any help."

She turned on him with a venomous glare in her eyes. "We're going that way anyway. It couldn't hurt to tag along with them. I wouldn't mind the company anyway."

The last part seemed to sting, turning the man's expression sour. She said it, Hank thought, in a way that suggested the guy with her wasn't very good company. He looked away to hide it. She ignored his reaction and turned back to face the others with the same smile as before.

"Well," Jennifer said, her first words. "The more the merrier!"

The old woman's smile grew. "Splendid!"

They started walking, and at first, it was mostly quiet between the newly formed group until the old woman turned around and broke the silence.

"I'm Eve, by the way. This is my husband, George. We're from Bangor. It's a little town in Maine. You probably wouldn't have heard of it. Jennifer is from there, too." Eve signaled at Jennifer.

Hank tried not to smile and stare. She was pretty. "Jennifer is, *was*, my daughter's best friend. She… she…" Eve paused, taking in a heavy breath. "Haley, my daughter, she died in a car accident five months ago."

"I'm sorry," Hank said amongst a flurry of condolences.

"It's…" She trailed off.

Hank thought the woman was going to say it was okay but stopped. He wanted right then to tell her he understood, to tell her about how he, too, lost someone, his wife, and his own life may as well have died along with hers, in a way. But he didn't because he didn't want it to seem like he was pulling the attention away from her, so he refrained.

"It was an accident. The roads were bad. It was nobody's fault."

She trailed off again. Hank imagined she was remembering the particular snowstorm that turned the roads into the deathtrap that took her daughter. It was nobody's fault. He didn't think she sounded as convinced of that fact as she wanted the others to be.

"But that's why we're here," she said. "Haley loved mountain climbing, but we were always too busy to tag along with her. You should always make sure you're never too busy for what's important because you could blink, and it will be too late."

Hank nodded. Charlie was smiling rudely, but Hank couldn't imagine what for and didn't want to ask him in front of these people. It looked like Scott had noticed, too, and was scowling at him.

When the silence seemed to hang for a while after Eve stopped talking, and he was absolutely sure she wasn't going to continue, Hank turned back toward the young couple hoping to break it.

"Where are you guys from?" he asked.

"Here, actually," the girl said. "I only live maybe two miles from here."

Hank noticed she didn't say "we," so the guy she was with likely didn't live with her. He told himself that this thought was random and that he wasn't interested in her in some strange, romantic way. His mind was just all over the place those days. That was it.

"My name is Jackie, in case you were wondering, and this is Jake."

Jake said nothing, not a greeting, nor did he offer where exactly he was from.

"We come up here hiking at least once a week. We try to more often, but unfortunately, life has a habit of getting in the way, you know? What about you?" she asked.

Hank glanced quickly at Eve first, as if worried his story would somehow upset her. Then he looked down at the ground, wondering if maybe he should just make some other story up about why they were there.

"My wife died a few months ago." He felt everyone's eyes move to him, but he couldn't lie. It would be an insult to Mary's name. "She…wasn't a hiker, nor was it an accident. It was cancer." He was still staring at the ground, afraid to look up and meet everybody's eyes. He knew how they would be looking at him. The same way they'd looked at Eve, and the same way everybody else had been looking at him for months. "It took her quickly. I barely felt like I had any time to say goodbye."

Eve came out of seemingly nowhere and wrapped her arms around him. She pressed him up against her tightly. A feeling of warmth washed through his body. It was as if this were the first hug he had received since his wife died that wasn't given just because it was supposed to be, because it was expected, but to take away the pain, to spread something like happiness from one person to another. She wanted to share his burden. He wrapped his arms around her and hugged her back.

When they released each other, everyone was still staring, but Hank didn't care. "I came up here just to clear my head, I guess. I couldn't continue on like life was somehow going to be normal, like the only thing that had changed was that I wasn't waking up to my wife anymore. As though life could march forward as if her subtraction meant nothing in the grand scheme. Because it did, God damn it! It meant…everything." He wiped a tear from his eye and started walking again. Everyone followed. He forced a smile and then met eyes with Eve. "And my name is

Hank." He chuckled softly, remembering now that he never gave it.

"I'm Scott," Scott said.

Charlie followed with his own name. At that, they let silence retake its hold, walking down the path that cut through the forest. The awkwardness was mostly gone, though. It was as if the two sorrows, the two tragedies that the group shared, somehow cancelled one another out.

"So, why did you guys pick this mountain?" Jackie asked.

"It was just the biggest one on this side of the mountain range," Hank said, glancing back at the couple walking behind him. "I also read that this one had a low difficulty rating, and this is my first major climb, so I figured this would be a good place to start."

"The end is why we chose this one," George said, one of the few times he had spoken since they all met. "Haley said the first ninety percent was a cinch compared to the end, and we want to make this climb count." He chuckled. "Making it one of her favorites. I suppose we'll see, won't we? This first part has been no cake walk either."

They continued beyond obstacle after obstacle, some more difficult to pass than others, all while the incline got steeper. Everything was getting a little wetter as well, the dirt trails soggier, as they drew closer to the top. They avoided, passively, discussing anything too sensitive. Most of the conversation was about what they did for jobs, what they enjoyed doing in their free time, and other things that most of them didn't really care much about. Eve knitted. Jackie read, a lot apparently. George worked on various building projects in his garage. Jake didn't do much, it seemed. Nothing he would forfeit at least. He was in a flag-football league with some friends during the summer, that much Jackie revealed. But she didn't reveal anything else when Jake shot her an annoyed glance. Hank told them about his job, making sure to leave out the part about him storming out and never going back, and about his near obsession with horror films. He had seen them all, it felt like.

Every once in a while, they would stop to take pictures. Eve said they were to mark the occasion, a sort of scrapbook for their first adventure into the mountains. They were already planning more outings despite not having completed their first yet. Eve listed some of the places they intended to go. Hank didn't recognize just about any of them aside from the Appalachian Trail, which he had heard of but knew little about. Their excitement was contagious, though, putting smiles on just about everyone's faces. Even Hanks, especially when Eve shared little anecdotes about her daughter's visits to some of the places. The only one that didn't seem to absorb even the slightest amount of it all was Jake, who hung back behind Jackie, wordlessly hiking along. Hank felt like the guy was brooding, what about, he couldn't guess. He was just a miserable person, he guessed.

Soon, the sun started lowering in the sky and the shadows of the trees and of the bushes and everything else grew longer. Darkness overtook places where light had once been. Hank glanced up to the sky and saw the sun's rays forcing their way through the thick tree cover, noticing how much darker everything had gotten in such a short time.

It was getting late. He pulled his cell phone from his pocket and checked the time. It was already early evening. Their frequent breaks were greatly extending the expected amount of time the climb should have taken. He didn't mind, though. He had nowhere else to be. And, honestly, each time they stopped, Hank was grateful. The soreness in his legs was unrelenting. Even though he, Scott, and Charlie had been taking turns carrying the tent, his legs didn't seem to be getting any rest in between.

They stopped again. Hank slid the straps off his shoulders and let the tent fall to the ground before leaning forward and letting out a great, deep breath. His heart rate was through the roof and his knees were beginning to feel like Jell-O.

"You know," Jake said, "people don't generally bring tents up here. These hikes don't take the whole day, usually," he shot a quick glance toward the old couple, but they didn't notice, "and the peaks get quite cold at night, even in the warm months. Only amateurs would bother with a tent."

Jackie shot a glare at him. "Jake!"

"I'm just saying, you look winded. You'd probably be fine if you hadn't brought that tent. Really, you'd probably be better off just leaving it here and picking it up on your way back through. The trail only gets worse from here. And at the end…well, you're going to have a tough time."

Charlie turned to Jake like he was ready to throw hands with him, but that didn't seem to faze the guy. Jake was right, though, Hank was an amateur, and he knew it. He wouldn't admit it, not to this guy, but he did regret bringing the tent. He would note the mistake for next time.

Hank didn't respond. He just focused on catching his breath and slowing his heart.

Jake laughed. "Keep carrying it. Suit yourself. I'm just trying to help."

Hank didn't think he was trying to help. It was more likely he was just looking for an excuse to be an asshole. Charlie backed down, finally breaking his stare on Jake. He and Scott looked just as tired as Hank felt. Hank was beginning to wonder what he was thinking trying to tackle a mountain like this. There were hills all over New York, he should have practiced on some of them before coming to a place like this. He felt way out of his league.

The old couple finally stood back up, which cued the rest of them to get up and get ready. Hank lifted the tent onto his back and started walking. Jake may have been a jerk, but he wasn't lying. It wasn't long at all before Hank noticed the incline growing even further. He tried to ignore it, sending the thought to the back of his mind.

"I'm bored," Jake said, sounding as though he were right behind Hank, finally eager to talk his mouth off. "Maybe we should tell some stories, some creepy ones. Hank said he likes that kind of thing. And these mountains have a life of their own. They've been here far longer than any of us have. Some say there are still undiscovered places and things out here, things…that want to be left alone."

Chapter 6

Things left undiscovered. Hank immediately thought of the human remains that were often found months or even years after a hiker went missing, if ever. All around him stood dense brush. He doubted that if he even walked twenty yards out into the unknown, he would be able to see back to the trail, back to the people he walked with now. He shivered, and not because of the temperature, even though it was slowly dropping into a colder realm as they moved up the hill and the sun began to take shelter.

Jake spoke in an almost hushed tone at first. "In 1973, there was this dude named Robert Garrow who came up here into the mountains and went on a killing spree." This turned a couple heads, but Hank didn't bite, not yet at least. "He pulled over on Route 8 near Speculator, New York, just a few miles south of where we are, actually, walked straight up to a campsite carrying a 0.30-caliber rifle, and pointed it at a young couple who were still laying down in their tent." He chuckled, getting a rise out of the looks everyone was giving him. "Rumor has it, they were still naked and everything. When their two friends came back from fishing, he made them all tie each other to trees and then he gutted one of them, one that had been getting mouthy with Garrow, and then left him there, his head dangling down on his chest, which is exactly how they found him later. They weren't the only ones Garrow killed either. It turned out that just days earlier he had killed another guy, Daniel Porter, and had taken Daniel's girlfriend Susan. God knows what he did to her."

Hank thought there was a sick enjoyment lingering in his words, as if he were not only enjoying the fear he hoped to instill in the others but was getting off on describing what had happened to the people. Was it an obsession? He knew all the names without a moment's hesitation, as if he had researched the subject thoroughly and had told the story many times before.

"Even before that, before Daniel," Jake continued, "he kidnapped a sixteen-year-old girl and murdered her. It's unknown exactly how many people he killed in his life. Some say it was close to thirty. And they still haven't caught him."

That turned everybody's heads, even Hank's, Charlie's, and Scott's. With all their eyes on him,

Jake's smile grew. He looked down at Jackie, who was already staring at him. Hank couldn't see her face, but she saw Jake's smile lose some of its luster.

"All right, fine," Jake said. "They did catch him, but he escaped jail and—"

"No," Jackie cut in. "He tried to escape from jail. They shot him. He's dead."

Jake groaned. "Why did you have to spoil it? Did you see their faces?"

Everyone turned away, each equally as ashamed as the next at how deeply they had been pulled into the story. Charlie looked a little pissed, but when didn't he? Hank thought.

"I was just trying to have a little fun," Jake mumbled. "We're walking one mile per hour over here. It's mind-numbing."

The talking ended. Maybe it was because everyone was exhausted or perhaps it was because they all were lost in their own little worlds of thought. Hank's eyes kept wandering off into the woods. The growing darkness was mesmerizing. At one point, he almost stepped off the trail, stopping himself right at the edge of the woods. It was no big deal, he told himself as he snapped out of it. But he had to be careful. Who knew where there might be drop-offs? But he couldn't help himself. The darkness, the mystery, which had overtaken most of the woods around him, enticed him, calling out to him with the allure of something secret, something hidden, that one could only discover by venturing out in the black. Was this what had happened to all the others? Who really knew what was out there, truly? How much of the deep terrain was still unexplored by man because it was just too dangerous to wander off the trail? How many bodies of those that dared were still lost?

Most of the people he had read about had disappeared in the modern era, but what about before that? What about in the 1800s or 1700s? How many were lost and unaccounted for, forgotten by history because there was nobody there to record their disappearance? He swallowed hard, a dry, nearly painful lump moving down his throat. How many would disappear in the future?

Every little sound in the woods caught his attention. Each twig that cracked, each bush getting blown about in the wind, every squawk and every buzz from an insect's fluttering wings. The whole thing reminded him of a movie he had watched one night weeks back about three people who went out into the woods to make a documentary for some project. It was for school or something; he couldn't really remember. But they were looking for a witch that was rumored in local lore to live out among the trees. Lost and mapless, the three kids each went a little crazy before ending up at some random rundown house in the middle of nowhere, which was where things ended. He wondered then if there were any random houses out in these woods, maybe an old hunting shack or something long untouched, the hinges on the door old and rusted, the windows covered in dust and cracked like a spider's web sprawling across the glass.

He hoped not.

He didn't think he could handle that. If they did come across something like that, what in the hell could they do? Turn and run? That sounded like a one-way ticket to getting lost and becoming the next victim on that long list of missing people.

They finally reached what Hank could only describe as literal hell. Before him was an obstacle, something that seemed to have been made for the gods. Rocks formed layer after layer of giant stairs leading toward the peak of the mountain, as if it were not humans that Mother Nature expected to be up this high but giants. His legs trembled with the soreness they had yet to suffer but would, undoubtedly, suffer soon.

"I guess your daughter was right," Hank muttered.

George stared up to the top, or what looked to be the top. "You ain't kidding."

Jake laughed. "Come on, it's not that bad. I've done it a hundred times."

Hank wanted to tell Jake to shut up, that not everybody was him, and that they got that he was some super-cool climber, but that outburst wouldn't solve much of anything, so he kept the thought to himself.

"Once we get to the top of this, we're home free, though," Jackie said. "Just a little further now."

Scott was staring up to the top and Charlie was staring at the base, where the stone stairs began, looking like he regretted making this trip more than anything else in the world. Hank couldn't say he didn't feel the same way just then. But just as Scott seemed to feel, staring up instead of down, to the end of their objective, to the finish line, he too wanted to finish, to accomplish this mountainous task. They had already come so far. He needed to do this.

He stepped forward first, lifting his leg up high and planting it at the top of the first rock, then lifted himself to the next level. He turned back around and faced the others, who were all moving now toward the rocks themselves. He could see clear over them, deep off into the woods, and in some places, even further, beyond the trees to the clear sky behind them. He was beginning to grasp then just how high they were. He had never been at that height in his life, not even on the coasters at the theme park his parents used to take him to when he was little. And he still had a way to go.

Charlie climbed up next to Hank with a quiet grunt, as did Scott. Jennifer had already started up without Hank even noticing and was helping Eve and George. Her arms were outstretched as she heaved George to the top of the first rock. Jackie and Jake both climbed up without a single sign of being so much as lightly tired. They didn't stop to wait for the others this time. With one quick glance from Jackie, probably to make sure nobody was dying yet, she and Jake continued up another layer of stones.

"I guess this will finally make us men," Hank joked as he pushed himself up another level.

Scott laughed, but Charlie was silent.

"What?" George asked.

Hank was surprised the old man had heard him even through the light breeze and exhaustion. He wiped sweat from his brow and took in a deep breath. "Nothing, I was just talking to this lot."

But George wasn't listening anymore. He was facing the other direction, listening to Jennifer talk about what, he could only imagine. That was fine, though, because he honestly didn't feel like he had the energy to both talk and climb at the same time.

For the first few minutes, it didn't seem all that bad. He wasn't in the worst shape, and it was pretty much just like climbing stairs, large stairs, granted, but still just stairs.

That was for the first few minutes.

After that, it hit him like a ton of bricks. It started with a warmth burning first around his knees, but then the painful heat spread rapidly throughout. The ache didn't wait long before it metastasized to the rest of his body as if he were not simply climbing with his legs but his arms as well, and his torso, and everything else. It was like a cancer.

And when he looked up to see how much further he had to go, he nearly passed out. He was barely beyond a quarter of the way there. He hunched over, his hands on his knees and let out an exhausted sigh that was so filled with agony that it was nearly a pout. There was a sickness deep within him, a lingering discomfort that he knew had spawned from exhaustion and would only grow if not tended to with rest, and soon.

Up ahead, he could see Jackie and Jake tackling the hill with finesse. George and Eve weren't even far behind him and the guys. He could barely beat out an old couple. The lingering question was rushing back with renewed vigor. What in the hell was he doing there? Trying to push away his depression by climbing a mountain, something in which he had no experience and no previous interest in doing up until just days prior? Not only did it sound stupid even to Hank, but almost juvenile as well. He could get hurt out there and for nothing more than a brief chance at feeling better?

"Come on," Charlie said.

Hank hadn't realized it, but in his moment of brooding, he had managed to fall a solid fifteen yards behind his friends and even a little way behind the old couple and Jennifer. He tried to hurry a bit, but it was easier said than done. He took in a deep breath, ignoring the pain in his legs, and pushed himself up another level.

When he looked up and saw Scott and Charlie still waiting for him ahead, the tent on Charlie's back, he felt renewed admiration for them. Neither looked all that beat, even with Charlie carrying the tent, he looked better. It was amazing. He, on the other hand, felt worse than he ever had, physically at least, in his entire damn life.

He pushed up another level, then another, until arriving at Scott and Charlie. Scott patted him on the back and continued up himself. Hank tried his best to stay in tow. The old couple and Jennifer were almost right alongside them. He was willing to bet that if George and Eve weren't there, Jennifer would already be at the top. She looked seasoned, even better off than Scott and Charlie who seemed surprisingly fine. Hell, even the old couple looked far better off than he felt.

He looked away, pushing the thought back. He didn't need to worry about how anybody else was doing except himself. They were almost halfway up now, or so it looked. If he just focused on the task at hand. He hoped to God it ended where he thought it did.

Annoying, buzzing insects kept landing on his sweaty skin, getting stuck and dying. His ears seemed to be their favorite location to do this. He tried to swat them all away, but he simply didn't have it in him. He shut them out, along with his negative thoughts, in a deep place, somewhere in the back of his mind where he hoped they would stay. He would do absolutely nothing but push until he reached the top, because if he stopped to do anything else, even to look back to see how far he had come or ahead to see how much further remained, he wasn't sure he would be able to start back up again.

Finally, he reached the top, stumbling to the ground as his foot reached up for another layer of stairs that weren't there. He let himself fall, hitting the ground dramatically in a conveniently located patch of grass. The landing wasn't hard. He rolled over and looked up into the clear sky, a light blue barely touched by scattered clouds, and let himself sink into momentary relaxation, so infinitely happy to finally be off his feet.

A gentle breeze touched his face on its way by. He heard steps near him but didn't care enough to turn his head and see who they belonged to because it didn't matter. He made it. He was at the top of the mountain. He had done the impossible.

He took in a deep breath. Off to the side was an opening, a cliff where the trees ended, and a beautiful view began. Even from where he lay on the ground, he could see clear off the cliff, into the distance, into a seemingly endless expanse of mountains.

"You just going to lay there for the rest of your life?" Scott asked.

Charlie laughed. "Only the strong will survive."

"Then I'm weak," Hank muttered, a smile weakly creasing his lips.

Scott extended his hand, and Hank took it, getting pulled up to his feet. When he turned around, he saw off the cliff from a new angle. He realized immediately, now that he wasn't on the ground, just how magical the sight really was. But he still wasn't truly at the top, not yet. When he turned around, he saw all the others entering a trail and disappearing from view.

"Guys!"

Scott and Charlie turned as Hank hurried toward them and the trail's opening. Seeing the others up further, Hank hurried by his friends to them. As soon as he reached them, the exhaustion came rushing back. He shouldn't have run. It was stupid. His body was still beyond exhausted. And it wasn't like the others were going to disappear. And if they did, for whatever silly reason, he still had Scott and Charlie.

The other two caught up, Scott with the tent on his back, Charlie with a weird smile on his face.

"You okay?" Hank asked, curious how Charlie looked so happy when Hank felt like he was about to fall the hell over.

Charlie smiled even wider. "Just excited, man!"

Everyone came to a stop at a tower. It was tall and wiry, ending at its peak with a small shack-like enclosure.

"It's the fire tower," Jackie said, seeing the confusion on Hank's face. "The idea is that if there is a fire up here, you can climb the tower to be safe. Though," she looked up toward the top, "I'm not so sure this old thing is going to keep anybody safe from anything. But, in other news, it is the best place to get a beautiful view."

She rounded the side of the tower and started up the stairs. Everyone followed. Hank was right behind her, but he was most focused on the old, rickety stairs at his feet and the general frailty of the tower. Wire fencing wrapped around all four sides, but there were so many gaps and holes in it that there looked to be less fencing than there was fencing. They went up level after level until they reached the tower's canopy where it was enclosed but also almost completely open on all sides with metal bars forming checkered windows that spanned it in three hundred sixty degrees.

Outside the tower was perhaps the most beautiful thing Hank had ever seen in his entire life, aside from his wife. He wasn't sure there was anything anybody could say in that moment that would convince him that the mountains didn't go on literally forever. The fear of being up so high faded in an instant. He saw layers of fog mysteriously tucked between the mountain crevasses. In the distance, the sun was beginning to take shelter behind the mountains, pitching an orange hue across the entire horizon.

Dark was beginning its reach its eerie tendrils across the fading sky, laying its blanket over the horizon, over the trees, and slowly, over everything else. Hank looked down over the edge and saw where frayed parts of the metal wire fencing poked out from the stairway. All the way down, the ground had already started morphing into an undulating darkness, a shadow caused by the trees but fed by the dying sun and encouraged by the coming night. He couldn't even see his bags and tent anymore, which he had set near the base of the tower. He hadn't been afraid of heights since he was a kid, but his stomach was suddenly spinning, and he felt light-headed.

He stepped back, grabbing a railing. Nobody seemed to notice amongst the excitement. He grasped the metal hard, not wanting to let go, afraid he would somehow end up over the edge if he did. He closed his eyes and focused, counting to five in his head. When he opened them, everything had finally slowed. The sky stopped spinning and life returned to his lungs.

"I'm gonna head down, I think," Hank said.

Scott was the only one to hear him apparently. He turned and nodded. "I'll go, too."

"Crazy, huh?" Scott said as he followed behind Hank on the stairs.

Hank glanced back but only just barely, afraid to take his eyes off his feet. "Huh?"

"The view, I mean, and us being up here. It's wild."

"Definitely," Hank said.

He had been distracted by the spiraling stairs. They seemed somehow steeper on the way down, the wiry fence even scarcer than before. He felt like he was going to trip at any second and go launching right off the side of the stairs, crashing to the earth with crippling, deadly force.

Relief washed over him as he took the final step onto solid ground. A couple others, the young couple, Jackie and Jake, Hank could hear heading down not far behind him, probably underwhelmed by the view they had already seen so many times before. The others were still at the top, their awe obvious by their repeating of how beautiful everything was. Sound carried better at these heights, and he could hear them clearly even from the ground. He smiled, perhaps for the first time since the climb had begun, at their infectious excitement.

Jake and Jackie were whispering amongst themselves as they joined Hank and the others at the bottom. When they stopped, Jake looked at Hank like the very sight of him had him ready to be sick. Jackie stared at her boyfriend like she was waiting for him to say something, but when a minute passed and he still hadn't, she spoke up.

"We don't think we'll have enough time to make it down the mountain before it gets dark."

Hank looked up at the sky. He had noticed the dark just as Jackie had, only he had failed to connect it to their return trip. Orange covered the horizon in creamy waves. Clouds were scarce, and sunlight was beginning to be as well. It wasn't *that* dark yet, but Hank could easily imagine how much darker it was amongst the thick tree-cover that lined the trails up. Looking off into the woods, he could already see the shadows growing darker, the visibility hiding away as if afraid of the dark itself. He didn't want to be out there once it became truly dark.

"And we didn't bring a flashlight," she continued.

"Because we shouldn't have needed one," Jake cut in, the contempt in his voice clear as day. "We should have been back down the mountain hours ago."

He didn't need to say more. Hank knew why the two of them were still up there. They were babysitting the rest of them. He wanted to apologize, but he couldn't because he wouldn't be able to stomach Jake's satisfaction.

"It doesn't matter why we're up here." She looked at Jake first and then Hank. "We're still up here and it's about to get dark, and quick. We have to decide what to do. Should we just spend the night up here then?"

Hank followed her gaze to the tent on the ground. He tried not to smile and not to look at Jake, instead diverting his attention to the ground as he fought to regain his composure. It may have been partially his fault that they were up there so late, but the glorious idea that his "amateur" tent was about to save the day was almost too much bear.

Hank looked up, catching Charlie out of the corner of his eye having a lot less luck holding his smile back. But they didn't seem to notice. "We can use the tent," Hank said. "There should be enough room inside for all of us, I think."

"Thanks," Jackie said.

"What's that about the tent?" George asked as he stepped down from the stairs, using the stair rail like a crutch.

"We're gonna stay up here tonight," Jackie said. "We can all share Hank's tent. I don't think we would make it down the mountain before it got too dark to see."

George did the same as Hank, first looking to the sky, then off the way they had come. "Hell, I can't even see right now. And I could really use a rest. My body is aching all over the place. I'm fine with staying up here tonight." He turned to his wife. "Are you?"

There was more doubt on Eve's face. Her eyes and her cheeks scrunched like someone was telling her an unwanted ghost story. "Is it safe? I mean, are there bears, or mountain lions, or anything like that?"

"Not likely," Jennifer said. "It's true when they say that they're more afraid of us than we are of them. With so many of us here, I doubt we'll have a problem. It does get a little cold up at these elevations at night, though." She directed her attention at Hank. "Probably a stupid question, but you didn't happen to bring a bunch of blankets, did you?"

Hank shook his head. "None, actually."

At least it would be fair, Hank thought. The last thing they needed was discord between the group over who got to use the blankets. It was a little dramatic, but *The Lord of the Flies* suddenly came to mind. It was a story about a group of kids surviving alone after becoming stranded on an island, and the chaos that ensued. It would take quite a while to reach those extremes, but he wasn't looking to spark anything.

Hank saw the disappointment and anguish in everybody's eyes. "At least we have the tent, though," he said, trying to force a nonexistent smile onto his face.

The tent didn't take long to set up. They had to get it done before night fell, so they did it as quick as possible. Even though he knew the size expectations, he was still pleased with how large it was now that he could see it set up. They would all fit in it at one time without a problem.

The sun was just barely peeking out from behind the mountains at that point, an orange sliver shedding nothing more than stray streaks across the darkening sky. Jake climbed into the tent without a word, Jackie trailing not far behind.

She turned to him as she went inside. "We're going to get some sleep now. We wanna get down the mountain bright and early tomorrow morning."

Eve overheard Jackie's words and agreed. Everyone was exhausted and a little eager to get off the mountain they hadn't planned on getting stuck on to begin with. Hank wasn't exactly tired in the sleeping sense, but he didn't have much to start a fire with, and even if he did, it seemed like everything was a little wet up that high. The entire ground was moist. The air was thick and wet. With what little camping skills he had, he doubted luck would be with him.

Hank turned and saw Scott standing a little way from the tent, staring off into the distance.

"What's up?" Hank asked as he walked up beside him.

"It's just…a little crazy, I think, standing out here miles from civilization, in the dark, lost amongst the trees. It's kind of surreal."

"I know what you mean," Hank said, looking up into the blue sky, which was just a few shades better lit than the world around it.

"The stars," Scott said. "You can actually see them out there. They're kind of beautiful."

"Gay."

They both turned around. Charlie stood there with a smirk on his face. "You guys going to kiss?"

"Wouldn't wanna get you off when we're about to share a tent," Scott said as he turned and started toward the tent. "Not my thing, buddy."

Charlie laughed. "I'm sure it's not."

Hank gave Charlie a look as he followed Scott toward the tent, tiredness finally creeping up on him. Charlie looked back and scoffed.

"What? I was only kidding."

Hank tossed and turned, but no matter which way he laid, he just couldn't get comfortable. The alcohol he had sipped before heading to sleep should have done the trick just as it had too many times before over the last few months, yet it hadn't. Not at all. There was just something about rocks jamming into his side, and his back, and everywhere else, that didn't sit well with his attempt to sleep. Eventually, he gave in and sat up.

Pitch black was all he could see in every direction. He searched around for his phone on the tent's nylon floor for a few seconds before finding it. He unlocked it and alive came the screen's light, chiseling through the dark. The light looked utterly out of place in the surrounding abyss. He hurriedly tilted it away from the others so he wouldn't wake anyone. The last thing he wanted was to plunge others into his waking hell of not being able to fall asleep, or back to sleep.

All around him was the soft, nocturnal chorus of crickets and cicadas chirping their night song. He wondered how dark it was outside now that the sun was fully gone, but he was far too afraid to venture out and check for himself. There, alone, he did not fake bravery, nor even consider doing something as crazy as leaving the confines of the tent. He assumed, then, that that was probably how a lot of those disappearance stories truly started: one person walking off alone when everything in the universe hinted that it was a bad idea. How many steps away, he wondered, would he have to go before he could turn around and not even be able to see the tent anymore?

"Can't sleep?"

Hank nearly jumped out of his own skin. Turning, he saw a figure at the other end of the tent, a mere outline formed from darkness in the vague shape of a human. He turned the phone and in its dim light reflecting off the tent's inner surface, the curves and wrinkles of Eve's aged face looked different— haunting, almost. Each contour seemed to have its own shadow. Her eyes looked blacker than he remembered. He knew the word, what exactly she reminded him of, but he didn't want to even think it. He remembered the college kids from that film, lost out in those woods in search of an urban legend, woods that seemed so similar to the woods they were in now.

"Hank?" she asked.

"No." He snapped out of the thought. "No, I couldn't sleep. These rocks—"

"I know what you mean. It feels like sleeping on a bed of nails."

He laughed, unsure if it was quite that bad. "Honestly, I don't rough it very often. I already miss my bed," he said.

"Me neither." She smiled, her teeth a fading yellow. "I don't think I'll be doing this again any time soon. I think my Haley would be proud enough. I don't know how she did this all the time."

Hank just nodded. Eve reached into her pocket and pulled something out, then extended her arm and passed it to him. He had to crawl like a ninja over to get it from her. Everyone around them was sleeping soundly, some of them snoring.

He turned the paper around and looked at it. It was a picture, a photograph, of a very pretty young woman, her hair long and blond, her eyes a bright green that Hank thought had to have been contacts. She wore glasses and a t-shirt and looked as carefree as somebody could. At the bottom, it read "Haley/2018." He smiled simply because, in the photo, she was smiling, and it was so bright, and charming, and infectious, that her smile spread to him through time and space. He knew it was a rude thought, but he almost couldn't believe a girl so pretty could die, as if beauty was a shield. If that were true, Mary would still be alive.

"She's pretty," he said.

Eve's smile grew, glowing, as she reached for the picture. He handed it back, and she look a long, deep look at it. He could see the pain there; even after years of it waning away, it was still there, and it would likely never go away. It eroded your soul. He imagined that must be what his eyes looked like when others looked at him. The eyes, he thought, that must be where the pain lived, where it seeded and where it grew, that and the heart, both of which died eventually, too.

He reached for his bag, unzipping it quietly, and dug his hand into the contents, searching for the cold glass bottle. It was calling to him, the drink, and he wanted to answer. He had a feeling he would need it, lots of it, if he hoped to get any sleep that night.

Hank pushed open the front door, kicked off his shoes, and hung up his coat. Snow was just beginning to fall, and he had a dusting of it in his hair, but the heat of the house melted it all nearly on contact. He was exhausted, frustrated, and ready to sit on the couch and take a load off.

As he turned around, Mary came in a hurry down the stairs. She greeted him with a smile and hugged him.

"Well?" she asked, pulling her head back to see his face.

"Well, what?"

She shook her head, her eyebrows lifting, like his misunderstanding was just asinine. "The promotion? Did you get it?"

He stepped away from her and threw himself onto the couch, then yawned. He picked up the remote and turned the television on. The news came to life on the screen and he changed the channel, not wanting to deal with whatever crisis was going on in this chaotic world that day.

"Hank." She entered the living room behind him, her hands on her hips, frustration brimming the curves of the once-smiling face. He wondered then if the smile she had greeted him with had even been real, or just some ploy to get his guard down. "Are you going to answer me?" she asked.

"No," he said, returning his eyes to the television. He didn't need to see the look in her eyes any longer, the disdain that had grown there.

"No, what?" she pushed. "No, you aren't going to answer, or no, you didn't get the promotion?"

"No," he said, refusing to take his eyes off the television. "I did not get the promotion. And can I not have five minutes of peace before you start in on me?"

She threw her hands up. "Why? Why didn't you get it?"

He snatched the remote up from the couch and turned the television off. He paused for a long moment, listening to his wife's heavy breathing and feeling her anger resonating. He considered what to say, wondering what string of words would bring the conversation to an end the quickest.

"Too late."

"Too late?" She stepped forward, now nearly hovering over him as he sat on the couch.

"Mark applied before me. He got it." His eyes remained ahead, still imagining the emotions flaring in her eyes, the ones that had spawned over the last few months, or maybe longer, growing into something so different than the spark he remembered seeing in her eyes on that day he had brought her coffee.

"Are you kidding me? I told you to apply earlier. I told you this might happen, and you didn't care."

He finally looked up at her but didn't say a word. She stared at him, not necessarily expecting him to say anything, but sort of assessing him, he thought. Sizing him up. He watched as her face cringed, changing shape, as if she couldn't decide what to do or what to say, as if her brain itself were overheating and was nearing shutdown.

Finally, she turned and stormed off, back toward the stairs, surely heading up to their bedroom. She spent an increasingly significant amount of time up there those days, but somehow, he just didn't care that much. She could take herself and her judgement up there with her and be mad, alone. He was tired of it.

He was too exhausted from work to let himself stress after hours.

Did she not think he was disappointed as well? He really did think he would land the promotion without a sweat. He knew that Mark had applied before him, but Hank was one-year his senior there and had put in hard work, and dedication, all while sticking around at the place for the past few years while many others had come and gone.

All the overtime. All the sucking up to a boss he didn't even like. Loyalty meant nothing. Hard work meant nothing. He needed the raise. *They* needed the raise. They were renting this house, but the owners were poised to sell, and they wanted to get into their own home. That would have been entirely possible if he had gotten the promotion.

But he hadn't. And now they wouldn't be able to get a house of their own. Was it his fault? He knew Mary thought so. She let it slip one day when they were arguing, when things got really heated. She had pointed out how well paying the job had been that she had left behind to be with Hank and how she would have gotten plenty of raises and potentially promotions by now had she stayed. She made a lot now where she worked, but it just wasn't enough for a decent house in the area they lived in.

He knew she felt terrible about herself after she had calmed down, after the argument was over and they'd both had the time to think. But that damage had already been done. She was considering if the trade had been worth it, her job for him. Could he blame her, though? He had been chasing advancements for years now and had accomplished nearly nothing. In secret, he often found himself disappointed in himself, too, feeling like his life was going nowhere.

She would be up there right then, doing something on her laptop, one of her shows playing on the bedroom television. Maybe she would be checking her messages. If she could go back, would she take up his offer for coffee? Would she even respond to his message that day at the office?

Something deep down told him that she wouldn't.

Light glared into Hank's eyes. That seemed to be the only way it went lately. He tried to swat it away, but his efforts fell short. Even through his eyelids, the light shined brightly, like the sun was waiting, and burning, just outside them. Finally, he sat forward, a little annoyed that the tent was so transparent.

But it wasn't the sun. It wasn't even day. Scott sat over him, the light from his phone blaring into Hank's eyes.

"What the hell are you doing?"

"You gotta wake up, man!" Scott said.

Hank was furious for a moment. He had finally fallen asleep, and now there was Scott, waking him up with a goddamned light jammed in his face. Especially with how hard Hank tried not to wake anybody earlier when he himself couldn't sleep. He fought the urge to sock Scott in the face.

But the anger passed when he realized that everybody else was up, too, and they were in a panic. He pushed himself up to a better position. People were peeking out the tent, leaving it, coming back in and out like they were playing a game of musical tent.

"What's going on?" Hank asked.

He took in his surroundings. Charlie was gone, outside the tent with the others, he assumed. Jackie and Jake were outside as well; he could hear their muffled talking. Eve and George were still inside, and so was Jennifer. They were talking quietly right then, over in the corner amongst themselves.

"You have to go outside and see," Scott said.

There was a look in Scott's eyes, fear, maybe, that really brought Hank to attention. Hank crawled on all fours over to the entrance. As he pushed the tent door flap to the side and climbed out, he was greeted by darkness, the same darkness he had seen and felt before falling asleep. Charlie, Jackie, and Jake stood there. Jake and Jackie had been talking but stopped when they heard Hank approaching.

Hank had expected to see meteors falling from the sky or something and was a little annoyed when there wasn't. "What's happening? Why is everybody freaking out?"

"The darkness," Jackie said.

Hank's eyebrow lifted. "The darkness? That tends to happen at night."

"That's just it," she continued. "It's not night, not anymore."

He didn't understand what she meant. Of course it was night.

She saw his confusion. "Look at the time. Look at your phone."

Hank pulled his phone from his pocket and looked. At first, he didn't really understand what he was seeing. The clock on his phone said it was seven in the morning. But that couldn't be right. Unless the mountains got lighter later, but that didn't make much sense either. How could it be seven in the morning and still look as black as night? That's when he noticed it, the sky, the black sky, and the complete absence of both the stars and the moon.

Chapter 7

Nothing was quite the same as it had been before he'd fallen asleep, he saw that now. The darkness…it was…he couldn't even explain it. It just seemed…darker. The stars were gone, but that could just mean there was cloud cover. He looked down at his phone's clock once more, hoping to see something different this time.

He didn't.

It was still about seven in the morning. But how? And, to make matters worse, he didn't have any phone service at all. Just to be sure that he wasn't imagining all of this, he dialed his mother's number and pressed the phone to his ears. His foot tapped anxiously on its own while he waited to hear a ring.

Nothing happened.

It just said *CALLING MOM* on the screen, but no ring came, only silence.

Hank shook his head. "I don't understand," he mumbled, looking down at his phone, at the time displayed on the screen, at the time that simply had to be false. There was no other explanation. "How can it be dark if it's morning?"

"That's exactly the problem, dipshit," Jake snapped.

"Jake!" Jackie snapped back. "Don't be an asshole!"

Jake grumbled under his breath before turning to Hank. "Sorry, I'm just…"

"It's fine," Hank said, understanding the guy's frustration while also already knowing that the dude *was* in fact quite the asshole. "Maybe…" His words trailed off as he stared into the distance, somehow able to see the outline of other peaks across the sky despite the moon and stars being gone. "Maybe it's always like this up in the mountains."

"No," Jennifer said from behind him. He turned around to face her. "I've been up all of these mountains, every single one of them, some multiple times, including this one, and never have I experienced anything like this."

"She's right," Jackie said. "We've been up here many times as well and never…never had we experienced anything like this."

"But you said yourself that you don't spend the night up here, so you haven't been here this early."

That didn't matter and he knew it. There was a long pause, a moment of silence as the entire group stood there contemplating. Hank considered the situation, trying to come up with the best course of action, even though he knew that, of everyone there, he was probably the least qualified to make any decisions up there in the mountains.

"I think that," Hank started, staring down as to not meet anyone's gaze, afraid he would lose his nerve, "maybe we should just wait here for a little while, just to see if it starts getting light again. Maybe there's like…an eclipse going on or something. I don't know. But I'm sure that, maybe, if we just wait a little while, it will start to get light out."

"I agree," Eve said, a small line of fear outlining her words. "There must be a reason for this. If we wait, maybe the sun will come out. It has to."

Someone agreeing with him knocked a weight off his chest. He let a breath out and almost smiled. "Right," he said. "We can wait, just for a little bit."

Nobody disagreed, not even Jake. What other option did they have? Proceeding down the mountain in this dark would be incredibly dangerous. So they would wait and hope.

Hank started dismantling the tent along with Scott and Charlie. Jake joined in begrudgingly after Jackie whispered something into his ear. Once done, they waited, some of them sitting on the ground, others standing against trees. Hank kept staring off into the distance, hoping to see the orange hue of the sun approaching the backside of the mountain.

But it didn't happen. By the time Jake stood up in anger, Hank could see a lot better than he could before, his eyes having adjusted to the surrounding darkness.

"This is dumb," Jake said. "It's not getting any lighter. We've killed over an hour sitting around, doing nothing. I don't know what in the hell is going on here, but what I do know is that we need to get the hell off this damn mountain."

Jake glared daggers at everyone, one by one, as if daring anybody to argue back. But nobody did because now that they had waited, now that time had passed and the sun was still nowhere to be seen, descending the mountain really was their only option. They hadn't brought enough supplies to survive up there for any prolonged amount of time.

Hank nodded. "He's right. I don't understand what's happening either, but whatever it is, it's not good, and it's definitely not normal. I think we should get down this mountain as quick as we can."

Eve was practically shaking when she stepped forward. "But…but how will we make it down in this dark?"

Jake started speaking, surely to say something rude, but Hank cut him off. "We just have to, Eve. There's really no other option, I don't think. We don't have much food or water up here. We couldn't make it for long."

Eve's gaze diverted to the ground. George looked like he wanted to say something but didn't. Hank's words, as grim as they were, were true. They had to be said. George stepped toward his wife, touching her on the small of her back, he whispered something soft to her, then she looked up and gave him a peck on the lips.

"We should go then," Jackie said.

The trail was like a dark tunnel as the group started their way away from the former camp site, their phone flashlights beaming ahead through the thick, inky darkness. Each member remained close to the others, the blackness around them absolute. Hank barely dared to even look off to the side, away from the beams of light, in fear that he would somehow drift off in that direction and be consumed.

This darkness was anything but natural, that much Hank was absolutely sure of. He tried to keep a strong face in front of the others, when there was still the smallest of chances that whatever was happening was just some kind of…mistake, but deep down, he always knew, somehow, that the darkness was not going to go away just by waiting.

He remembered the path as they walked back the way they came. They arrived back at the clearing where he had fallen to the ground for a rest the previous night, so thankful to have made it to the top of the rock stairs. Thankful to even be alive. Ahead, he saw the clearing, the cliff where the forest finally ended, if only for a second, to give way to something infinite.

He approached it slowly, remembering the drop-off and fearing it in the dark, fearing the possibility that he may not see where the land came to an end. When he did reach the edge, he stared off into the distance, at a sight that seemed strange because he didn't remember it being there before, on their way up. There were lights, tons of them, on the ground maybe a couple miles from where they stood. Around them, he could just barely make out the dark outline of structures. Buildings, or houses maybe, he couldn't really tell. The lights flickered in a way that added to the strangeness because normal lights didn't flicker, not unless they were about to go out, that is. Hank wasn't sure now, as he stared at them, that they even were lights.

"This doesn't make sense," Jackie said. "There shouldn't be a town right there. There *isn't* a town down there."

The lights were flames, torches or something, Hank realized. That's why they appeared to be flickering. It could have been a camp, a very large one, but its size told him that wasn't the case. But if it were a town, why was it lit by torches and not electricity?

"What the fuck is going on?" Jake said, not to anyone specific.

Eve was talking in hushed tones to Jennifer, who stood there wide-eyed, staring toward the town herself. "What is happening, Jennifer? Was that town there before?"

"No," Jennifer answered. "It wasn't. It isn't. They're right, there is no town right next to Snowy, especially not in that direction. There should only be woods there."

Hank wasn't sure what any of this meant. How could all of them have missed that little town on their way up? He supposed none of them really stopped that long at the cliff, not long enough to notice something like that so far away. It wouldn't have been lit up, likely blending right in with the trees and everything else.

"But it is there," Hank said. "We can all see it. Whether or not it was there before, it's there now."

"I think we should keep going," Jackie said. "I think we should go now."

"Yes," Jennifer said, shooting a glance at the old couple she had accompanied there. "We need to get going."

Nobody was about to argue. Everyone, even Charlie, looked a little scared. And Hank couldn't remember a single time, ever, that Charlie was afraid of anything. Jackie and Jake started walking, and they all followed, their steps a little quicker now.

Hank was not excited at all about the prospect of descending the stone stairs in the dark. He could imagine making one wrong step, tripping and stumbling down them, then landing at the bottom in a crumpled heap.

"What do you think it is?" Jackie whispered to Jake just up ahead of Hank.

He listened carefully, knowing that they were trying to be secretive but curious what they really thought. He glanced back, wondering if the others could hear. None of them seemed to be aware but him.

"I don't know. But it can't be a town. There isn't a town down there," Jake said.

Hank tried to speed up a little, barely able to hear the couple's quiet words.

"This might sound a little crazy, but what if it's like some sort of cult or something?" Jackie asked.

Jake took a long moment before responding. "That's not any crazier than anything else that's going on, I guess. I don't know if it's a cult, and I don't really want to know. Let's just steer well clear of it."

Hank couldn't believe what he was hearing. He was glad then that nobody else had heard. A cult, the idea was terrifying, especially out in the woods like they were. Scott and Charlie were just behind him talking amongst themselves, the other three further back. Hank could just barely make out Jennifer's consoling words as she tried to comfort the old couple to little avail.

"We'll get down the hill just fine, I know it," she said. "I'm sure there is a reason for this. We'll be fine."

Words that Hank knew weren't completely true. Words said in hope rather than in truth. They'll be *fine*.

"We'll go straight to the police. They'll have to know something."

Hank almost laughed at that bit. The police. As if those guys would have all the answers. Most of them barely had an education let alone an understanding of the cosmos, or whatever this was. They would have better luck heading over to the local college, if there was one, and asking the teachers there.

Jackie and Jake came to a sudden halt in front of Hank. Everyone piled up like a stopped train. Jackie was looking around, flashing her light into the surrounding woods, ahead of them, and even behind them. She circled around to the back and just stood there for a moment.

"I—" She shook her head. "I don't understand. We should have reached the stone stairs by now."

Hank realized this right as she was saying it, completing her thought just moments before the words came flooding from her mouth. They should have reached those wretched stairs a long time ago. They were located just before the clearing. It should have taken them mere seconds to reach them. Yet they had been walking for minutes now and had seen no sign of them.

Hank turned around three hundred sixty degrees, panic mounting within him. Eve let out a sob that seemed sudden in the otherwise silent forest. George pulled in his wife for a hug but didn't say anything because there was nothing that could be said. Jake, on the other hand, had plenty to say, letting out curse word after curse word before turning away from everybody else.

Jackie rested her head in her hand like she had a headache. "This—this just can't be. It makes no damn sense. First the lights down the mountain, now the stone stairs are gone. It's like we're on an entirely different mountain or something."

"We can't be," Scott said behind him.

Hank turned toward his friends.

"But we have to be," Charlie replied.

Hank's eyes drifted back to the darkness, in the direction they would need to continue in, because they had no other choice, and wondered what kind of sick nightmare this was.

Chapter 8

It wasn't long before they continued their walk. They couldn't just sit around wondering. It was already clear that waiting wasn't going to accomplish anything. Each group had begun their own side conversations again, all of them in whispers as if coming up with their own secret plans to escape this dark fantasy world.

    Hank stopped, looking off into the woods to his left. In that direction, if it were real, was the town, or whatever those flames had been. He imagined a small village with houses made of logs where people lived in seclusion, not having made contact with the outside world in generations, where they worshipped ancient gods and made sacrifices to appease them. As outsiders, they, of course, would be the sacrifices. That's how the movies went, at least.

A chill slithered down Hank's spine, not because he was afraid, even though he was, at least a little, but because it seemed to be getting colder rather than warmer as the dark day dragged itself forward in time.

"Do you think it's out there?" Scott asked.

Hank hesitated, unsure of how to answer.

"Yes," Charlie answered, taking the words right out of Hank's as he was about to say them. "I mean, we all saw it."

Scott nodded, his eyes not meeting the others'. Hank could tell the guy was more shaken by all this than he was willing to let on. But Charlie, on the other hand, he had a smirk on his face, as if all of this was somehow amusing.

Charlie was about to say something else when there was a noise. Hank turned quickly, looking into the darkness, into the direction they had come from. He was expecting to see Jennifer and the old couple, but they had already passed. In fact, the rest of the group was almost out of sight already in the seconds Hank was stopped. The sound came again, this time closer, but still in the dark, as if right in front of them but hidden behind a veil. The sound, as it repeated back in Hank's mind, sounded like a branch snapping under the weight of a step.

"Did you hear that?" Charlie asked.

"What are you doing?" Jackie called back.

Hank glanced her way for a second but didn't answer. He was listening carefully for whatever the sound was, wondering if it would return, hoping it would not. He swallowed hard, waiting fruitlessly.

"Hank, let's go!" Jackie and the others were walking back toward him now, their lights cutting their way through his darkness. "What are you doing?"

When Jackie stopped alongside Hank, she looked in the direction he was but didn't see anything, noticing the disgruntled look on Hank's face.

"What is it?" she asked, her words nearly a whisper.

"I thought I heard something."

She looked from Hank back into the empty void. "Like what? Like a bear?"

Hank just shook his head. He had no idea what he'd heard, nor if he had really heard anything at all. Given how far out in the woods they were, it was likely nothing more than a wild animal scampering through the brush, or even just a breeze blowing a branch in just the right way. That was what it had to be.

"It was nothing, probably. Just hearing things." He felt like he was telling a lie even though he had no reason.

"Don't lose yourself," Jackie said. "The situation is bad enough. We can't start seeing things. And we have to stick together. No more stopping without letting everybody else know. We don't need to be splitting up." Her smile was warming but her eyes were firm and demanding. His stopping, he thought, had frustrated her more than she was nice enough to say, and he understood why.

She turned around. "We have to get going."

He almost responded, "Why?" but stopped himself. It was a serious thought, though. Why did they have to be in a hurry? It wasn't like they had to get down the hill before dark; that ship had sailed and then some. It was a little cold but not enough to really hinder their travels. So, what reason did they have other than fear?

But fear was enough, he answered for himself. Fear was enough to make a person do a lot of things, like hear sounds in the woods and wonder if it was a monster even though he knew monsters didn't exist, not under the bed like he was afraid of when he was little and not here in these woods.

But there was plenty else to be afraid of, namely starvation and dehydration. The elements. Hungry wild animals.

He followed to keep up with the others, not wanting to lose track of them or push Jackie's buttons. Their flashlights lit the trail a pale yellow. The trail itself seemed to be barely there. On their way up, the trail was well defined, easy to keep track of. Now it was less like any of that and more like misplaced hope. Hank wondered if it even was a trail they were following or if it were just some clearing they decided to follow, digging themselves deeper into the endless Adirondacks.

There was very little talking, and when someone did talk, it was usually one person assuring another that as long as they pushed onward, downward, they would eventually reach the base of the mountain. When they weren't talking, everybody was staring off into the woods as if expecting a bear to jump out at any moment. Jackie was in the lead, everyone else following in tow. Hank and some of the others had already decided to rotate flashlight usage. Only half of them needed their lights on at once; otherwise, they were just wasting battery.

When Jennifer suggested they conserve their batteries, Hank thought Eve was going to break into a fit. Her eyes went white, and her face grew pale white.

She stuttered, her eyes glossing. "But, but, why? We're not going to be up here long. The trip up wasn't that long. It shouldn't. I mean, we will be down soon. There's no need, no need at all. We couldn't run out of battery that quickly, and we need to be able to see where we're going."

But George calmly removed the cell phone from his wife's hand and then gave her a soft kiss on her forehead. She didn't scream back at him, not like Hank thought she may, but instead retreated, speechless and defeated. For a long time, she didn't say a single word, as if sleeping within herself.

"She going to be okay?" Hank asked Jennifer.

Jennifer glanced back at Eve, who was staring toward the ground, George's arm around her shoulders.

"I think so. This is just a lot for her, for both of them, for everybody, I guess. It was supposed to be a trip out to show their love for their daughter, to remember. Now…it's a nightmare."

Hank nodded. He knew how that felt. He was out there for a similar reason. This was supposed to be his chance to clear his head, to maybe move on in some way from the loss of his wife. There was so much he regretted. So much he would do over, do differently, if he could. Their relationship had so many ups but also too many downs. Perhaps it was because she was gone now, and going back was impossible, but it was all the bad times that seemed to shine the brightest in his memory. He would wake up all the time, hot, and sweating, having been rocked awake by some horrible memory magnified by sorrow and sadness, an event he knew hadn't been nearly as bad as he was recalling it.

"How did you know…Haley?"

In the gleam of Jennifer's light, he saw her smile at him having remembered the name. "Grade school," she said. "We were best friends. She was my *first* best friend. I was new. I didn't really have any friends where I'd come from, but Haley, she came right up to me on the first day of school and introduced herself. Honestly, at first, I thought maybe she was just doing it to be funny, you know, 'Haha let's pretend to be friends with the new girl,' but no…nobody was watching. She just wanted to be my friend. She was…genuine."

Hank smiled, but only half-heartedly. He never really had a friend like that. Sure, he had Scott and Charlie now, but he hadn't known them for all that long. As a matter of fact, he could scarcely even remember when or how he had met them. He looked at them, then, Scott and Charlie, and wondered what they were thinking. Scott was scanning the tree lines, staying aware and vigilant, readying himself for God only knew. Charlie, on the other hand, was looking at Jennifer as she spoke to Hank, listening but saying nothing. He had grown far less talkative than he had been, surely lost somewhere in his own mind, wondering what in the hell was going on around them. That's what Hank was thinking about at least, somewhere in the back of his mind, even as he engaged with Jennifer, even as he listened to her story. Nothing about what was happening was natural. He couldn't shake it.

"We stayed friends all throughout middle school and high school and even after we graduated. We became roommates and went to the local community college together. And…" Jennifer suddenly let out a soft sob, cupping her face in her hands to choke down the sound. When she came back up, she was relieved to see that nobody other than Hank had noticed the momentary breakdown. "I'm sorry," she said. "I just haven't really talked about any of this with anybody but George and Eve."

"No, it's fine. It really is. I understand, sort of."

Her eyes widened. "Yes! I'm sorry," she said again, "I'd totally forgotten about your loss. I'm sorry if…"

Hank shook his head. "No. It's fine, really. That's why we're out here, isn't it? To get it all off our chests? To find some semblance of peace? Or try to, at least."

"I suppose you're right." She looked up at him. "How did you meet your wife?"

Hank laughed. "It was a mistake, actually. We met over messaging, at work. We had like this group chat thing for the office, and she was in it, and so was I. Well, one day, the boss had sent out a message to everybody and she accidentally responded specifically to me."

"Accident, huh?" She giggled.

"Really, it was. We'd never met. I had no idea who she was. But I replied. It was the best decision of my life."

"And just like that, you guys were married?"

"Well, not quite. We dated a while. Then…pretty much, yeah." His grin was wide and proud, still surprised to this day that such a beautiful, perfect woman had picked him to spend her life with, down to the last second, despite how little he deserved it at times.

"I think she was probably a lucky girl," Jennifer said.

Hank nearly laughed but held it in. "I think she was probably just in it for the coffee."

"Coffee?"

"Nothing, just a thing. Not important."

His smile had faded. She didn't respond. He felt bad but was relieved when she finally fell back after a long bout of silence, to check on George and Eve. Ahead, Hank could hear Jackie and Jake bickering but about what, he had no idea. They were whispering so quietly their voices could have been in his head. But whatever they were talking about, the conversation came to a heated stop, and Jackie took a step away from Jake. It was only a single step, but it was likely enough to get the point across.

Hank, Scott, and Charlie fell back in together.

Charlie spoke, looking both ways first to make sure nobody else was listening. "I don't like this," he said. "This isn't right. I keep thinking that I'm seeing things in the woods, like out of the corner of my eyes, but when I look…nothing. Ever."

Hank looked into the woods off to his left, focusing, attempting to shut out everything else. There was a slight breeze that came and went, shaking the branches and their leaves. But other than that, he heard nothing. The same off to his right and everywhere else. Perhaps Charlie was just being paranoid, listening for noises that weren't really there, his imagination hoping for them even.

Hank shook his head. "I don't know, man. I'm not seeing anything."

"You will," Charlie said, undeterred. "You will."

Chapter

9

George had been the first to suggest that they should stop and maybe set up camp, but Hank was fairly certain it was on behalf of Eve. They had been walking for hours on end with very few rests but hadn't reached the bottom of the mountain still. Eve looked totally winded, and so did everyone else. If the clock on Hank's phone was correct, it was approaching nightfall again, except, in this case, the sun never rose.

Now that they were preparing to stop, the weight of Hank's bags, and the pain they were causing on his legs, suddenly swooped back in. His mind had been so occupied with everything else that it seemed to have disconnected communication with that portion of his brain until just then. He heaved the bag off his back and let it drop to the ground, letting out a loud groan as he did so.

"You don't have to carry that bag alone," Jennifer said. "I can take it for a bit next time."

He smiled. "It's fine. I'm not."

He bent over to unzip the bag, reaching in to pull the ropes and pegs out. When he glanced back up, Jennifer was looking Jake's way, confused. She pointed toward him as if to ask something, but just as she did, he turned and walked over toward them. Without a word, he plunged his hands into the bag and began helping Hank set up. Hank was surprised, but something told him he wasn't helping out of the kindness of his heart. Hank wanted, for a moment, to double down on how Jake should be thankful that he brought the tent but decided against it again, not wanting to upset Jackie and wanting to be the better man. Sometimes being the better man really sucked.

With the tent set up, most everybody fanned out and started looking for kindling to start a fire. George and Eve spoke to Jennifer for a few minutes before retreating to the tent. Their distress was obvious, and Hank couldn't help but mourn the occasion. Hank handed off the lighter and fluid he had packed to Jackie, who thanked him with a smile. Jake scowled as the transfer took place. Hank could laugh, he thought. Another precaution paying off. Now they would have a fire, all thanks to his overplanning.

The fire was a bitch to start with all the mountain moisture in the air, but with effort, they pulled it off. In triumph, Hank had pulled out his bottle of Vavoom and sipped it, enjoying the soothing burn, when he noticed everybody else staring at him with desire. Everyone was happy to take a sip, to try out Hank's fancy-looking drink, to take off some of the edge if that was even possible, but nobody indulged, not heavily. Sitting around the fire, Jackie peeked over to the tent in silence, the bottle in her hand and an orchestra of crickets chirping in the background.

Jennifer, sitting closest to the tent, her arms wrapped hugging herself in the still-cooling night, caught her glance. "They're asleep. I can hear George snoring." She laughed.

"I think I have the answer to an age-old question," Hank said, a smile already growing on his face.

Everyone turned to him in confusion, sudden seriousness etched into them.

"If a tree falls and no one is around to hear it, does it make a sound?" He chuckled to himself. "Doesn't matter. You wouldn't hear it over the god damned crickets anyways."

Nobody laughed, but that didn't matter to Hank, because his smile still hung end-to-end across his face as he retold the joke to himself in his head, laughing internally all the while. Jennifer, Hank noticed when he took in the group's unhappy faces, was smiling, just a little, but Hank was endlessly pleased that it was there. The smile, he thought, which he had barely seen since they had met but could now see in the light of the fire, was glowing, and beautiful. He wasn't sure he had thought anything was beautiful in this life since his wife had passed. Pretty, maybe, he supposed, but not beautiful. Pretty was one, totally different, thing. He thought Jackie was pretty, maybe even gorgeous, the moment he saw her. She had every physical feature a man could want in a woman. Jennifer, too. But beautiful was something else altogether. Something you couldn't describe or quantify. It was magical. He didn't know why Jennifer was smiling, perhaps it was his joke, but he doubted it. But whatever the reason was, it was refreshing, and he hoped against everything that it would remain there, gracing Jennifer's face.

It didn't. The smile faded seconds later when Jackie suddenly began to talk, pulling him out of his euphoric daydream.

"I know we already talked about this, briefly, but does anybody have any ideas, any at all, about what in the hell could be going on?" Jackie asked quietly, taking another quick glance toward the tent as the question came out.

He knew why Jackie kept looking toward the tent. It was Eve. Everybody had been acting abnormally subdued about the situation. Nobody was panicking. That was almost more concerning to him. It was like everybody there thought that this was a passing storm, something that came in with bad weather, or a bad day, and would disappear at any moment, as if driving out from under the rain cloud into a sunny day. But Eve, she wasn't bothering with whatever the rest of them were doing. She was acting on the outside how everybody else had to have been feeling on the inside. She would go from calm, to mildly frantic, to crying into George's shoulders all within minutes, then return back to normal again. It reminded him of the stages of grief. Because that's what it was, wasn't it? Only she wasn't afraid to hide it. She had already gone through enough pain in her life; he knew all too well.

She was acting like it was the end of the world. And what if it was? What if it was dark like this everywhere? He wondered what would happen to the world if the sun died, or if the moon was gone, wishing he had paid more attention to Mr. Tanibom in science class.

Hank looked to Scott and Charlie but neither seemed poised to speak. He didn't have much of a clue either, aside from his burnt-out sun theory, but even he knew how dumb that would probably sound. Hank just shook his head.

"Alaska is dark months out of the year," Jennifer said. "I went climbing there once. It has something to do with the earth's axis, I think."

"So, you think maybe that Earth tilted or something?" Jackie asked.

"I—" Jennifer looked away, toward the crackling fire, which lit everybody's faces a slight orange hue. "I don't know. Could that even happen?"

Everybody looked to those next to them, then across, wondering if anybody had answers, and knowing that they themselves did not, because none of them were scientists. Hank was just a desk guy. What he did was of little importance and just about anybody could do it. He was very likely replaced at the office already by someone that had just as little knowledge about the world as he did. If the world were to end, if the sun went out, or if the world tilted and something awful happened, he would not be one of those people that were saved on the ship or on the ark, to repopulate and build the new world. He would be left behind to watch the old world die, him along with it.

"I don't know," Jackie said. "We're still here. So, whatever this is, whatever happened, it couldn't have been that bad."

Or maybe the worst of it just hadn't reached them yet. Maybe once they all fell asleep, they wouldn't wake back up. Perhaps, even, their bodies would be burned to ash or frozen solid, or maybe launched into space by some axis-related loss of gravity. He thought there was no moon. But what if the moon had really gotten so close to the Earth that it was blocking everything out? The tides would rise. Maybe the Earth would flood. He wasn't sure. The possibilities were basically endless, far beyond what his own mind could comprehend.

"We can't know that," Jake said, breaking his staring silence. "This is fucked up. There's no other way to describe it. This shit is so far beyond messed up. It can't even be real."

"What do you mean?" Jackie asked.

"I don't know. Maybe it's like some sort of group hallucination." He looked toward the clear bottle of alcohol, which had now made its way back around to Jennifer. "Maybe we ate something or drank something. Our minds aren't working right."

"I don't think so," Jackie said. "We haven't shared anything, aside from right now, and this whole thing didn't start just now."

Nobody responded, not even Jake, because there was little to say. Hank could see everybody digging deep into their own minds, trying to find logic where there was none, trying to come up with an excuse as to what was happening, any at all, but he could see it in their eyes that there was nothing.

That's when Hank heard Charlie's stomach growl loud enough that he was surprised when nobody looked up. Hank could relate, though. His stomach was starting to hurt as well. Nobody else had brought food, he was pretty sure, because none of them had planned on being up there any prolonged amount of time. They hadn't either, Hank and them, not more than the night, at least. They had some energy bars packed away in their bags, but outside of that, they had nothing.

Flashes, images of cannibalism, and being lost deep within the woods, shot through Hank's minds, lines from the stories he read, tales of missing people, dead people, and murders. He wondered then about what would happen if they couldn't find their way down soon, when everybody started getting hungry and if they found out that they were the only ones with food. What would they do? Would they try and take it from them? He wasn't sure any of them could overpower the three of them.

It wouldn't come to that. Hank wasn't a bad guy. He didn't want any of that. He would share if it came down to it. He could partition the food up. It was easy for him to think that now when he wasn't that hungry yet.

Beyond that, though. What would happen? After the food was gone and after they all failed at hunting because none of them, that he knew of, were experienced hunters that could catch a wild animal without a weapon, then what? Even with a weapon, Hank was almost certain he would be worthless in the hunt. He couldn't kill, not a deer, or a rabbit, and certainly not a human.

Cannibalism. His stomach rumbled and he tried to act like it didn't happen, afraid to look up and meet anybody's eyes, afraid that they had heard it and that their stomachs were doing the same.

Fear could make you do a lot of things, like think there was a monster under your bed, or make you hear sounds in the woods that weren't there. And maybe fear could make you do even worse things, especially when you're desperate, and hungry, and didn't know what else to do. Maybe then you would scrape the flesh from your own friends' bones.

"I think I'm going to head to sleep," Jackie said, signaling to Jake for him to get up as well. "Who knows how long it will take us to get down the mountain tomorrow? We should rest while we can."

If, Hank thought, loud enough that, for a moment, he worried that he may have actually spoken the words. *If* they made it down the mountain. But he hadn't, and the thought remained in his head where it was born and where it needed to stay. Dark figures passed over the scenery in a wave as the two crossed in front of the fire, two shadows pitching across a forest full, endlessly, of other shadows. They unzipped the tent and climbed in, leaving the sound of rustling nylon behind them as they situated themselves inside.

Charlie and Scott followed them inside minutes later, both stating how tired they were and how the other two were right about needing to get some sleep. Hank nodded to them as they disappeared. Seconds later, the silence returned, leaving only Hank there sitting in front of the fire, Jennifer not far away, the crackling and sparks of the fire bringing a flicker of light to dancing life against the trees and the sound of crickets singing everywhere else.

He stared into the fire, into the chaos that it was, and let the sight draw him into another place. It was bright, crackling in orange and yellow, burning away at what it was fed. When Mary was still there, they sometimes had little fires in their backyard. It was just them. Nobody else was there. Nobody was invited. They just hung out and let the fire take them away. They didn't need to talk. And sometimes, they didn't want to talk. And near the end, before she was gone, before his life had been consumed like the logs by the fire, he would let those flames take him back to a better time, a time when coffee brought them together and when their possibilities were not only happy but infinite and all things were possible.

"I really don't understand this," Jennifer said, pulling him from his trance, out of his memories. "It just isn't right. It can't—" She paused, looking up from the fire, into his eyes, bringing the fire with her, and giving it to him in her stare. Her eyes flickered. "It can't be real."

"Yet it is. It's all real," he said, the chorus of chirping almost loud enough to bury his quiet words, bury them deep under, where everything else that was dead lived.

Hank was jolted awake by a sound, twigs snapping, he thought, like back on the trail earlier in the day. Only this time it had been louder, enough so that it had woken him from his exhausted slumber. He sat up, finding himself outside, next to a dying fire, its coals burning away their last bits of life. He must have fallen asleep there. Except he didn't remember doing so. Jennifer was gone, the spot where she had been sitting vacant. He couldn't recall her telling him goodnight either.

Had he fallen asleep that quickly, that heavily? Twigs snapped again, not far away. He jumped to his feet, taking a step back as he did so, away from the sound. Instinctively, his eyes kept snapping toward the tent, toward backup. Bushes shuffled. The air was icy.

He was about to make a break for the tent when a voice spoke from beyond the veil. "Hank," it whispered, low, and sweet, and familiar. "Hank, come home."

He shook his head. It couldn't be. It was impossible. She was gone. She was…

"Haaannkkk."

It sounded so close. He leaned a step forward, his heart pounding, trying to see beyond the darkness, even if only barely, because that was where the whisper was coming from. Not from far out, an echo lost somewhere in the distance, but from right in front of him. If only the fire had a little more life left in it, its light may have reached further. He was sure if it did, he would be able to see.

"Hank," the voice came again. "Help me. Please."

He swallowed dryly, almost painfully, and whispered back, shaking, "I can't. I— I— You can't be here. You just can't. You— You're—"

The words kept choking up in his throat, his thoughts tangled and disoriented. His eyes brimmed with a glossy layer of tears. A quiet sob escaped from within.

"Why are you doing this to me?" he said, the words so quiet that they almost weren't even there.

"Stop," the voice said back. Only this time it sounded different. It didn't sound sad any longer. It sounded…angry. "Stop!"

It screamed, an awful, guttural shriek that ripped at his ears. The shrubs shuffled violently, and he finally made a break for the tent. He grabbed the little zipper and yanked it, feeling the presence right behind him, right on top of him.

He dove through the tent's opening, landing on the grass with a hard thump. For a second, he twisted in surprised pain, groaning. It took his mind a split second to piece together what had just happened. He sprung back to his feet, looking all around. Where the tent should have been was an old, battered wooden door, creaking quietly on rusted hinges, a stench wafting out that could only be described as wretched and absolute. He stepped back, away from the tattered shack, fighting back the acidic gag that was rushing up his throat. He crouched forward and gagged, but nothing came out.

He rose, pulling in a deep, cool breath. An orange hue lit the trees around him, only, when he turned around, he saw that it wasn't from the campfire as he had expected. Torches lined the area, spaced almost evenly around a center where small structures sat, huts of some sort. There were tons of torches, a hundred, maybe more, scattered everywhere. He couldn't count them all and his head spun when he tried to.

There was nobody outside, but he could hear a distant mumble, a cacophony of hidden voices.

"Help me," a voice whimpered. "Somebody, please."

The voice spoke as if it were everywhere all at once. Hank hurried forward, rushing toward the first structure. As he approached, he saw that it looked primitive. The walls were wooden, made of logs and other tree debris, but also old pieces, as if the houses were built from things scavenged from a junkyard. There were no windows.

Grabbing the door handle, which was barely more than a sturdy piece of wood itself, he ripped the door open and rushed inside. People sat around a table, digging into a meal that he couldn't identify. It was mush in a bowl. They slurped and munched. The smell, the same smell that he had previously encountered at the shack, lived there as well, just not quite as densely, as if this stuff, whatever they were eating, had come from that place.

Small torches lined the inside of the house as well. Hank couldn't help but think of how dangerous that was, a wooden house, probably made from dry, fallen trees, lined on the inside by torches. None of them looked up at him as he watched; they all just ate and ate, as if this were their first meal in ages.

"Where is she?" he asked, afraid but knowing he had little time.

They didn't answer. They didn't even acknowledge his presence.

"I need to find her," he said, more urgently.

Then they turned, all of them at one time, their hideous faces coming to life in the light. Only centuries of inbreeding and pure, unadulterated hatred from God could have caused such grotesque deformities to spawn. A chunk of the grime fell from one of their mouths. He would have turned away, he wanted to even, but something about it was just so freakish that he couldn't. That's when he noticed the masks on the walls. Some of them resembled animals; others resembled things he could not identify. They were all painted in some tribal manner.

As they stared at him, the lights seemed to get brighter, more blinding, until he was forced to look away from the abominations.

"Why are they so bright?" Hank asked. "Why are there so many torches everywhere?"

There was a laugh, then an old woman's voice spoke. "Why, to keep the dark away, of course."

"What's wrong with the dark?"

A woman stood, the chair creaking beneath her, her face blinded out by the light. She did not step forward nor attack him like he had expected, but he stepped away instinctively anyway.

"Everything."

He paused for a moment, unsure of what she meant, confused by her and by the light that seemed impossibly bright now, as if it were trying to push him out of the house.

He held his hand up in front of his eyes. "Have you seen a girl come through here? A woman, dark hair, my height." He struggled to describe her, to come up with words, any words, with the light barreling down on him like the sun. "I heard her screaming."

"Yes," the woman said. "She had gone."

Hank recalled the scream, the terror in her voice. Her words, her cries for help. He didn't believe she had simply gone, not willingly. She would never leave them. She would never leave him.

"What do you mean, she left?"

"She left long ago," the woman continued. Then her arm lifted, and she pointed at the door. "As must you."

Hank wasted no time in leaving, following the woman's direction out the way he came. He hurried on to the next hut, desperate for answers. He pulled the door open, being met by another group of people sitting around a table, eating the goop without a shred of regard for the intruder.

"Have you seen a girl?" he asked without hesitation.

Small eyes tilted away from their meal to meet his own. A small, bald, decrepit man spoke with a hiss, as if his intrusion was annoying but expected.

"She has left. She is gone."

He bolted from the place, checking each building as he went. He suffered the same results at each until he was ready to give up, the inhabitants of each house growing more and more frustrated with his presence until the final one was downright hostile.

An old woman rose from her chair, her face mangled beyond what could be natural, and looked at him with her wandering eyes. "You are nothing but a fool," she said. "A fool from the darkness. A fool consumed by the darkness. And you must leave this place!"

She pushed toward him, forcing him out the door without a touch. The voice was identical to the woman in the first house. He stumbled back into the grassy field, barely holding his balance. When he regained himself, he froze. All of them, every person he had seen within the huts, were now standing outside, a whole crowd, all of them with those masks on, the ones that were hanging on the walls.

They were facing him, staring at him from behind the masks. He waited for them to come closer, to rush him, but after seconds passed, they still remained in place, hideous, terrifying statues.

"Help!"

He jerked around. In the distance, at the very edge of the light, the trees to her back, stood a girl. He squinted, stepping closer, trying to make out who it was.

"Please, Hank," she yelled. The voice, it wasn't the same person as before, or was it? He could no longer remember. "Please, someone help me!"

He sprinted toward her. She was just standing there, a statue like all the others. Then, just as he was about to reach her, just as he had gotten close enough to see that it was Jennifer, she let out one last scream, which was cut off midway by a terrible shriek.

Suddenly, her legs were torn out from under her. She fell straight to the ground, face first, with a painful thud. She reached for him, laying on her stomach, begging soundlessly. Then, before he could even react, before he could even think, in one single terrible instant, she was pulled into the darkness.

Hank let out a scream, despair and fear fleeing his body like it needed to paint the world. Everyone sprung awake, Hank's fear infecting them as they struggled in the dark to find their bearings.

"What's going on?" Jackie said, feeling for her phone, bringing the tent into light seconds later.

Hank sat there at the center of the tent, tears flooding his eyes, his face red and contorted. He looked at Jackie, returning her confusion. He felt the nylon under his hands instead of dirt as he leaned forward, sobbing deeply.

"What's wrong?" Eve asked. "Why are you screaming?"

"Probably a nightmare," George whispered to his wife. "Just a nightmare."

"All right. All right," Jackie said. "Let's get out of the tent. It's tight in here. Let's get outside."

They climbed out in single file, Hank going somewhere in the middle, George last, just behind Eve.

"Hank," Jackie said. "You were just having a bad dream, I think. You're okay now. Just relax."

Hank looked around, the fire burning with its last breath, just as he remembered, the coals just barely clinging to life. He searched the faces of those around him, all of them pale with shock from being awoken so suddenly. But he couldn't find her.

That's when Jackie noticed the same thing Hank was noticing. She counted the people around her, then spoke, her words haunting.

"Where's Jennifer?"

Chapter 10

Everyone started looking around as if each of them had just seen Jennifer standing alongside them a second earlier. But there was nobody else there, nobody besides Hank, Scott, Charlie, Jackie, Jake, Eve, and George. Everybody was silent. He could almost hear the pulsing throb of everyone's combined, rushing hearts.

"She must still be in the tent," Eve said, turning away from George to go check.

She swatted the door open like an annoying fly but couldn't see into the tent's darkness. She had left her phone inside.

"George, please, do you have your phone?"

"Yes. Yes." He pulled out his phone and handed it to Eve.

She clicked the button, bringing the phone's torch to life. Light filled the tent, scanning across its interior with the movement of her wrist, from one end of the empty tent to the other. She leaned inside, as if Jennifer could have been hiding in some unseen corner. After a long minute passed, George finally put his hand on her shoulder and motioned her out. Hank thought she would fight him, but she didn't.

"Well, she must be around here somewhere. Maybe she went off to pee." Eve turned to face the woods. "Jennifer!" she shouted, stepping closer to the trees. "Jennifer! Where are you? Please. Jennifer! Come out!"

Everyone joined in with the calls, everybody shouting in different directions. Hank just watched, a sadness running through his veins. It was like talking to a frantic mother more than forty-eight hours after her child had gone missing, knowing that the child's chances of returning were next to nothing at that point. His heart throbbed wildly as he recalled the bits and pieces, the tiny fragments of what remained of his dream. People in huts. Screams. Jennifer getting pulled away into the darkness. An unholy shriek that could not possibly be human.

Scott noticed Hank standing there, at attention, staring off into the woods, not shouting like the others. He stopped, too, turning to face his friend. But he did not speak. Hank could see in Scott's eyes a sort of knowing. They were close in those ways. He knew right then that Scott knew. Maybe not exactly, but he knew something was wrong, something far beyond what the others were imagining. Charlie, on the other hand, had been as silent as Hank, staring toward the trees right where Hank had been seconds earlier, probably searching for whatever Hank had been focused on.

Eve began sobbing, her words choking as tears ran down her cheeks. "Jennifer, please come back! Wherever you are, please!"

"Jennifer!" George called out. It was the loudest Hank had ever heard the old man speak. "Jennifer!"

Jackie was so close to the darkness as she shouted into the forest, "Jen! Jen, follow my voice if you can hear me!"

It looked like Jake had already given up. He didn't look sad, though. No, he looked angry, like Jennifer's disappearance was more of an inconvenience than anything else. He touched Jackie's shoulder and whispered something. Hank couldn't read his lips in the dark. The two of them turned to face Eve and George, who hadn't noticed yet that they were the only two left yelling. Eve took in a breath to scream again but gagged on air instead, her throat having run dry with exhaustion.

She pulled back to try and force another scream when Jackie stepped in. "Eve," she said, cutting off the old woman, drawing the older woman's attention momentarily away from the dark forest around them.

"You're going to hurt yourself," Jackie said, tears at the brink, her ability to hold them back quickly crumbling, "if you keep shouting."

This was a first. Hank had only seen the hardened side of Jackie, the side that told him to keep up the day before. Or at least he thought it had been the day before. It was damn near impossible to tell when it was out there. Minutes blended into hours, into days.

"Hurt myself?" Eve repeated, as if the words made no sense at all.

"If she were going to hear us," Jackie had her hands held up as if she were talking a gun out of Eve's hands, "she would have by now. Throwing your voice out isn't going to help things."

"What are you saying?" she asked, venom in her voice. "My voice," she stuttered. "My voice is the last thing that matters."

"I'm only saying that wherever she is, she must be too far out to hear us."

"I'm not so sure," George said. "These mountains go on for miles. Shouts echo. It may just be that she hasn't gotten here yet."

Jackie sighed, knowing just as Hank did, and all the others, just how unlikely that was. Why would she have been so far out? That's what Jackie wanted to say but wouldn't.

"I know what you're saying," George continued. "But we have to try. Jennifer has to be out there somewhere. She wouldn't just give up on us."

Eve stepped forward. "What if she heard us? What if George is right? What if she was following our voices back when you made us stop just now? And now she is waiting for us to shout again, so she knows where to go."

Jackie just stared at her. There was no right response to that. It was unlikely. If she could hear them, then it was just as likely that they could hear her. And if that was the case, why wouldn't Jennifer be shouting back so they know she could hear them? Wouldn't they hear her right then, screaming for them to keep yelling?

She couldn't break their hearts even further. Instead, she caved, averting her gaze away from the frantic couple.

"Maybe you're right," she said.

Jake went to whisper something else in her ear when she pulled away. "What do you want me to do?" she shouted.

"I don't know," he said, loud enough for Hank to hear as if he really did want to speak quietly but was unable to or unwilling to anymore. "But we—"

"What if we get the fire going and search the area, check for clues? Maybe there's a sign of where she went," Hank said. "It could be a good place to start. Maybe she'll even see the fire."

He felt like a liar, a terrible, ugly liar. But he wasn't. What he had seen really was just a dream, after all. Jennifer's disappearance wasn't absolute. Jackie nodded, looking to the others. Everyone was in agreement. Jake began searching the area for flammables while Jackie poked at the fire, trying to resurrect it from beyond the grave. It flickered, orange and yellow sparks dancing upward with each jab, but it fought back, refusing to come to life without the proper feeding. Jake tossed some dry leaves into the meager flames. Hank was surprised he found them given how wet the top of the mountain had been. Did that mean they really were heading toward the bottom, heading in the right direction?

He hoped. That was all he or any of the others could do, hope. The leaves caught fire and leapt into quick flames before burning out in an instant.

"More," Jackie said. "Find more."

Jake returned to the edge of the darkness where he had retrieved the other leaves, coming back quickly with another handful. They lit instantly, only this time, so did the charred log above the flames. Jackie had stabbed enough life into the loads of leaves that something began to rise from the ashes. Seconds later, there was a small fire. It flickered at first, then burst upward.

Light brought their surroundings into clarity. They could see each other now, much better than before. It was like a dome, Hank thought, a dome of light keeping the darkness out. Just like…just like in his dream. Everybody split up to search for clues but stayed nearby on Jackie's command. Nobody was to leave the immediate area. Everybody was to stay where others could see them. But Hank wasn't listening because his eyes had subconsciously found the same spot he had been staring at not long ago. Only now, he thought he knew why he had been staring right there, in that exact place, in the first place. They were the same trees, the same formation, he had seen in his dream, at the edge of the strange village, at the edge of the light. It was where Jennifer had stood.

Hank wasn't sure how long he had stood there. Long enough for him to hear Jake whisper quietly to Jackie that they should just give up, that they wouldn't find anything out there in that dark, that it was pointless. Hank stepped forward, wordlessly, toward the forest, toward where the light ended, and the darkness began. Someone mentioned, in the background of everything, to search for footprints or anything else that might tell them which way Jennifer had gone.

Hank paused for only a second, at the edge, where the fire and its light ended, before stepping across the black threshold. Small weeds and other brush scraped against his jeans as he pushed in deeper, not stopping nor slowing, but also not in any hurry. Because somewhere deep within his mind, maybe even his soul, he knew where it was, the thing he was looking for, and that it wasn't going anywhere.

When he came to a stop, he looked down at the ground. A single glimmer twinkled at his feet where the echoes of the fire's light reflected off glass. He reached down and picked up the camera that he remembered had been around Jennifer's neck earlier that day, the one she had used to take pictures of the mountains and all their beauty. He stared at it for a very long moment, feeling the cold plastic in his hands, wishing he hadn't found it, wishing that his dream had been nothing but that.

"Hank?" someone called out.

He turned and hurried back to the fire, considering for just a second that he should maybe drop the camera and lie that he had simply needed to pee, knowing just how much pain his discovery would cause. Everyone jumped as he came hurrying back into the light, all except Scott and Charlie, who had seen him disappear. They stared at him, camera in hand.

"I found this in the woods," Hank said.

He reached out and handed it to Eve. She examined it, wide eyed. He saw, they all saw, as realization grew in her eyes, along with another wave of dread-stricken tears.

"It's hers," she mumbled, the words nearly choked silent by a sob. "It's—"

She turned quickly, burying her face into George. He put his arm around her and squeezed her in. With the other, he took the camera from her shaking hand and held it out for Jackie to take.

Jake glowered at it in his girlfriend's hand, then he looked up at Hank. "How did you know it was out there?"

"What do you mean?" Hank asked.

Jake gently took the camera from Jackie's hand and approached Hank, deviance engraved in his face, a devilish half smile moving ever so slightly closer. He held it up for Hank to see in the flame's light.

"How far out there did you find this?" He raised his voice, magnified by the utter silence around them. "How in the hell did you know it was out there? You can't see shit. None of us can. Yet you walk out into the woods and come back with Jennifer's camera." He paused, giving the words a minute to linger. "Almost as if you put it there yourself."

"Jake!" Jackie yelled.

But he just held his hand up toward her. "Not this time. This creep knows something, or did something, and he's going to tell us. Right the fuck now!"

Hank stepped back. "Jake, I don't know. I—I just saw it there."

"You just saw it?"

Jake was about to push toward him further when Jackie grabbed him and pulled him back. He whirled around like he was going to swing on her but stopped.

"Jake, you need to stop!"

He pushed away from her and then turned back at Hank. This time, though, he did not advance on him. He lifted his finger in the air and pointed at Hank like he wished it was the sharpest dagger on Earth. "I think you did this, somehow. From now on, I'm not letting you out of my sight."

But Hank didn't know anything. He knew his dream, that was it. He didn't know where that dream had come from or how in the world it had translated into real life. And he couldn't exactly tell any of them that.

Eve had taken her head out of George's chest and was staring at Hank, not with accusation but with confusion. She must have been wondering the exact same thing Jake had been now that he had mentioned it. Everyone's eyes were on him and there wasn't a single thing he could do about it because if he told them the truth, told them about his dream…if he told them that he had seen her at the edge of a small village, the village, he believed, that they had seen earlier from atop the mountain, if he told them that something had grabbed her and pulled her into the forest...

They would think he was insane.

Chapter 11

We have to wait. We have to give her a chance to come back. We can't go yet. That was what Eve insisted, what she said between stutters and whimpers, twenty minutes or so earlier. Now they all sat there, staring off their own ways, all lost in their thoughts, their eyes searching the dark forest. Everybody had been a little afraid before, but now they were jumping at even the slightest sounds, the slightest movements.

Eve had begun humming to herself, a soft sound that, if Hank were being honest, made everything a lot creepier. He wanted her to stop, to ask her to stop, but knew it would only get her going again. She had finally calmed down for the first time since they all woke up, or at least had gotten quieter and stopped crying.

Hank was considering his dream again. Like all dreams, it was fading further from his memory with every passing second. He imagined the torches, lining the outside of the village like a fence, and the huts, built from logs and trees like those inhabiting them knew nothing of nails. But those weren't even the worst parts. Their faces, their horrible, deformed faces, were what brought goose bumps to the surface of his flesh. Was it inbreeding? It didn't matter. They only existed in his mind, in his dreams.

Or did they?

They had all seen the village earlier. They had agreed, as one, to avoid it. He kept glancing toward Scott and Charlie. He wanted desperately to talk to them about it, to tell them about his dream and about how he knew where to look for Jennifer. But he couldn't, not without looking suspicious and drawing even more attention to himself.

And even if he could, would they, too, think he was crazy? What he was truly afraid of was that if he told them about the dream, they would join in thinking he had something to do with Jennifer's disappearance. Would Scott and Charlie turn on him as well? They were all he had out there. He didn't think they would, but under the circumstances, he couldn't be sure. Nothing was for sure, not anymore.

Jennifer's disappearance. Hank knew it wasn't simply a disappearance. She wasn't *missing*. She was murdered. She was dead. There was something in the woods. He had heard it before, twigs snapping under its feet. It lurked within the darkness. It took Jennifer, dragging her screaming to an untimely death. He was almost sure of it.

Jake was staring at him but stopped when Hank looked up. He wondered what the hot head was thinking. Probably about punching him in the face if he had to guess. If it came down to it, Hank wondered if he could beat the guy in a fist fight. Hank wasn't large, but he wasn't small by any means either. He wasn't some tough brawler, but he hadn't lost any of the fights he had been in back in school. Some were draws but none losses. He had Scott and Charlie there to back him as well, he hoped.

"She should be here any second," Eve said aloud. "Yes. Any second now, I think."

Jake groaned audibly. It was a bit rude, Hank thought, even heartless. Scott came over and sat beside Hank. Seconds after, Charlie followed suit.

"What do you think?" Scott asked.

Hank shook his head, unsure of how much to say, but relieved he asked. "I'm not very confident that Jennifer is coming back," he whispered. "I think something happened to her."

Scott leaned in. "Like what?"

Charlie hadn't said anything yet but looked as interested as Scott. Hank risked a glance toward Jake. It didn't look like the asshole was listening in. Hank took in a deep breath.

"I…" He swallowed hard, the moment of truth coming in a rising wave. If Scott and Charlie turned on him… "I—"

"Had a dream?" Scott finished.

Hank's eyes went wide. "Did you, too?" Hank could barely contain his relief. Perhaps he wasn't crazy after all.

"I did," Scott said. "We both did."

Hank's head snapped to Charlie. His friend nodded, his lips straight and his eyes tired. It looked like Charlie hadn't slept in ages. Hank almost smiled, though. He couldn't believe his ears. You never know how badly you didn't want to be crazy until you found out you weren't, he guessed.

"Then maybe everybody had the dream," Hank said.

Scott was going to say something but hesitated. "Maybe. But I don't think we should risk it," he said. "If we ask them about it, even if they did have the same dream, some of them may not admit it. Jake definitely not."

He was right, Hank thought. Jake would deny it just out of spite. Jackie might admit it. Eve, on the other hand…he was surprised she hadn't said something about it already, if it were true, if they had all had the dream.

"I think we should wait it out," Scott continued. "We should just wait and see what happens."

"All right," Hank agreed, halfheartedly, knowing it was the best thing to do but desperate, still, to prove his innocence.

It was beginning to get cold again. The fire had begun to die back down. Soon, it would be out if someone didn't tend to it. But adding to it would be deciding we would stay longer.

"I think we should get going," Jake said suddenly.

Eve stood up. "What? What do you mean?"

"Eve." He walked toward her slowly. "I want Jennifer to come back," he said, surprisingly calm. "But if she were going to come back, I think she would have done it by now, wouldn't she? If she was close by enough, wouldn't she have heard us calling out? Wouldn't she have seen the fire?"

Eve went to talk, but he cut her off. "I'm not saying she's… I'm not saying she's dead or something. I'm just saying that we can't stay here forever. I wish we could, but it's getting colder. Who knows how long it will take us to get to the bottom? We can't wait any longer. We have to go."

Hank laughed.

Jake turned to him. "You got something to say?"

Again, Hank hadn't meant to laugh out loud, only this time…he did. "I just thought it was a bit funny. You were accusing me earlier, acting like this was somehow my fault, but you are the one that wanted to give up the search so quickly earlier. You want to leave Jennifer behind."

Hank's words were cold and harsh and a little dishonest. He already knew that Jennifer was gone, and he mostly agreed with Jake on them having to leave, but Jake was an asshole, a world-class one at that, and he couldn't pass up the chance to get a good jab at him, even if it were at an awful time.

Jake looked baffled, taken aback. Impossibly, the guy looked speechless. "No," he said, almost as if it were a standalone explanation. "What the hell are you talking about? I didn't give up searching quickly. It has been like twenty minutes."

That took Hank by surprise. He started to say something but stopped himself. He was pretty sure it had only been a few minutes, less even, maybe, that he had been staring at the tree formation before entering the darkness to find Jennifer's camera. But if Jake was right…

"I agree." Jackie stepped forward. "I agree that we should start going." She turned to Eve, sorrow carved into her voice. "Look, Eve, I get it, I really do. I don't want to leave Jennifer. I don't. But what can we do? We can't exactly go searching the woods. We'd get lost. And, as Jake said, it's getting cold, and we are losing time. We need to get off this mountain. We need to, and now."

"You don't think we can hear you over there?" Jake asked, staring at Hank with nothing short of hatred. "You and your fucking whispering."

Hank was about to ask what in the hell Jake thought he and Scott were doing—conspiring?—when Eve started crying. She tried to talk, but her words were cut out by tearful chokes.

"Are you sure we can't stay longer?" George asked. "I think, maybe, maybe she's almost back."

"Back from where, though?" Jackie asked. "If we had any idea…any idea at all…"

"We're not leaving," Eve finally said. "You people can go, but we're staying. We're not abandoning her."

"Eve," George said.

"No!" Eve cut him off. "They can leave, but we're not going anywhere. What if she comes back here and can't find the campsite? What if she can't find us because we left?"

"Eve…please…" Jackie said. "Don't do this. Come with us."

"I can't." Eve sat back down, diverting her eyes away from everybody else. "I won't."

George looked on, looked at them all, with defeat, then, without another word, took a seat on the ground next to his wife. There was a long moment where everybody just stood there, like they were all thinking that this couldn't possibly be happening, that the two of them weren't really going to stay there alone.

Jackie walked over to Hank. Jake reached out like he was going to stop her from going anywhere near him but changed his mind at the last second, withdrawing his arm.

"Hank, please, can they keep your tent? If they're going to stay here," she sniffled and wiped a tear from her eye, "if they're going to stay here, then they'll need shelter. They'll need it more than us, I think." She whispered the next thing. "They're older, Hank."

Hank nodded his approval even though he didn't want to. They were old, yes. But it was their decision to stay there. Them being old and needing a tent wouldn't make the rest of them need a tent any less. He wanted his tent. Perhaps it was selfish, but Hank didn't think so. It was self-preservation.

"Great," Jackie said. She turned. "George, we're going to leave you guys the tent."

He looked up at her, not Hank, and thanked her.

Few words were said as they packed up their things. Hank was going to leave the tent but *only* the tent. He made sure to pack up all his gear, making sure that nobody saw the food he had. Then they stood there in front of George and Eve, ready to say goodbye. George stood and pulled Jackie into an embrace.

"Thank you," he repeated. "Truly."

When they broke apart, George still made no eye contact with Hank. That pretty much sealed it in his mind. George and Eve thought he did it, that he did something to Jennifer. He wanted to ask George about the dream before they left, but he wasn't going to. Hank recalled the terrible shriek echoing out from within the darkness, the shriek of whatever demonic creature, whatever beast or witch, took Jennifer and shuddered, knowing that George thought that witch was him.

"Good luck," Hank managed to say. And he meant it, because he knew the truth, he knew that something took Jennifer, something terrible and sinister and evil, and once they were all gone, those two would be left vulnerable. Whatever was out there would come back.

He knew their fate.

Jackie picked at the fire with a stick and tossed a few more dry leaves and wood into the fire, getting it going just a little bit before grabbing her things. With their bags in hand, they turned away from George and Eve and began to walk, everybody looking back occasionally except Hank. He refused to dwell on the past, not like he had done all those months prior. It was the future, and getting down this mountain, that mattered now.

They entered the darkness with just five of them now and walked until the fire was nothing but a distant flicker.

Chapter
12

A shout cut through the quiet darkness like a razor through hot butter. At first, Hank thought it had been in his head, yet another trick played by the endless shadow that swallowed everything around them, or by whatever lived in it, until everybody else stopped suddenly and turned around.

The shout came again. The fire could still be seen in the distance, a single bright star in an otherwise absolute night sky.

"George," Jackie muttered. "Thank God."

There was no hesitation. Everybody started back toward the campsite as fast as they could manage with such little visibility. Hank's light bobbed up and down with his uneven steps. He would have felt like he was jogging down a void, into some black hole, had it not been for the upward incline and the exhaustion keeping him tied to reality.

Their jogs slowed to a fast walk when they didn't seem to be getting anywhere. They could hear George shouting and even see his bodily figure eclipsing the fire as he walked around. But as they hurried toward them, the distant, small, glow of the flame didn't seem to grow any bigger. Hank stopped and looked behind him, feeling a presence there, as if it were watching him, as if it were laughing.

"Hank, c'mon!" Jackie shouted. "Keep up!"

When Hank turned back around, they were almost to the fire. George was there, the fire behind him, casting a shadow over his face.

"You came back," he said, nearly in tears. "I wasn't sure if— I thought maybe you wouldn't turn back."

"No," Jackie said, reaching out to hug George. "Of course we'd come back."

Eve got up and was saying something to Jackie when Hank got that feeling again, as if the back of a cold, icy hand was resting on the nape of his neck. He whirled around, only to be greeted by nothing other than the darkness. Scott and Charlie were watching him, wondering, perhaps, what he was doing, what he was looking at. But the answer was…nothing. There was nothing there, nothing that he could see, at least.

"I'm sorry," Eve wept. "I'm so sorry. We, we have to come, I know. We can't stay here. I just— I don't—"

Jackie hugged Eve, ending her frantic rambling. "We understand. It's fine, really. There's no need to apologize. Nobody is blaming you."

"We'll start packing up the tent," Hank said, gesturing at Jake, Scott, and Charlie to come help him.

They hurried. Hank wasn't sure a tent had ever been put away so quickly in the history of mankind. Jake didn't seem angry that they had turned around, not like Hank would have expected, only anxious, and in a hurry to pack up and get out of there. Just as Jake had said he would be keeping an eye on him; Hank planned to keep an eye on Jake. He didn't trust him, not even a little. One moment, he was accusing Hank of things; the next, it looked like there were other things he was afraid of. Hank kept catching the guy looking around, his eyes darting in different directions, like he had seen something he wasn't mentioning to anybody else. He hurriedly stuffed the tent into the bag, not saying a word the whole time to any of them, not even Jackie.

"I'll carry the tent," Jake said, turning away from Hank before he could even respond.

At first, a flare of anger ignited in Hank as Jake carried the tent toward Jackie. He wasn't sure what in the hell the idiot thought he was going to do with it. Hank needed it just as much as the others. It wasn't like he could keep it to himself. He was about to protest when he remembered how sore his legs had been. Scott and Charlie looked at him as if they, too, were wondering how he were going to react. Charlie looked ready to fight. Scott just looked exhausted.

"If that guy wants to haul around a heavy bag, he can be my guest," Hank said, turning away from his friends.

"Got the tent," Jake said.

Jackie nodded. "Are we ready to go?"

George looked at Eve, then back at Jackie. "I think so."

Hank kicked out what remained of the campfire, spreading the ash and cinders across the dirt. Then it was dark again, their flashlights on, and they were walking.

Hank's cell phone was over half dead. He wanted to ask the others how theirs were doing but didn't want to add to the existing anxiety. It wasn't long after they walked away from the final, dying cinders that Hank started hearing things again. He tried to ignore them at first. *Just keep your head straight*, he told himself. *Ignore it and it will go away because it's not real.* The sounds weren't real. But even though everybody was walking ahead of him, he felt almost certain that somebody, or something else, was walking behind him. He could hear the heavy patter of steps and the crunch of dead foliage snapping beneath weight. He counted the steps and the pace in his head. It was definitely a person. It had to be.

That's when a sliver of his dream came rushing back like bolts of lightning. Those terrible tribal masks, or whatever they were. The people were so hideous and deformed, like something left behind in the fallout of a nuclear attack. So abominable that he could barely let his eyes linger on them for more than a few seconds before he felt like the sight itself was beginning to cause him actual physical pain. The masks, he wanted to assume, were to cover their faces because of how the people looked, but that didn't make a lot of sense. These people lived what seemed to be totally secluded lives. Nobody had come across them yet because nobody had been dumb enough to camp atop the mountain until Hank had come along.

Or maybe someone had seen them. Maybe a lot of people had come across the village over the years. Somebody must have camped up there before; they had to. It wasn't *that* crazy of an idea. He recalled all the missing people that had seemingly vanished without a trace. What if they didn't simply vanish…and what if there were other villages? Surely *somebody* would have seen them in a flyover, or somebody would have found them and made it out to tell the story.

Hank's heart plummeted even further when he recalled how the huts had been built. They were formed by logs and branches, the leaves still clinging to most of them. And the tops, the roofs, of the huts, he tried to remember but couldn't. Angrily, he cursed the fading of dreams. He wondered how many great ideas had come and gone because dreams took flight so quickly after waking. What he thought he remembered was that the roofs were covered in leaves, mimicking, he swallowed dryly, the tops of trees.

From above, the huts may have looked like trees and shrubbery, perfectly disguising them from aerial searchers. Hank's breathing accelerated as his mind suddenly rifled through possibilities, grotesque images, and horrible truths, forming in the crevasses of his mind's eye.

The people would have to kill anybody who came across the village if they were to keep it a secret.

They lived in the middle of nowhere, so food had to have been scarce.

Living alone, living secluded, they wouldn't have the same laws or the same morals as the modern world.

His stomach lurched and twisted with approaching sickness as Hank struggled with everything that was spawning in his head. He tried to force away the thoughts, but his attempts were weak and futile. Behind him, even though he was lost in thought, he could still hear the footsteps. They didn't seem to be gaining on him nor falling behind, just continuing in almost perfect step with his own. He closed his eyes hard, forcing feeling back into his body. The darkness behind his eyes mirrored the darkness around them perfectly.

They ate them.

He opened his eyes, breathing a wave of cool, icy air into his lungs. If this village had somehow remained a secret for this long. If nobody ever escaped. And if these people were savage, and feral, and starving, then…they would eat anybody who discovered them.

That was the thought he had been pushing. That was the truth he didn't want to admit. Nobody ever escaped because they all ended up digested in their stomachs. Hank remember the mush he had seen them eating. Was it made from other hikers?

No, he thought to himself, still hearing the steps behind him. That couldn't be right. Had they grown closer? What would he see if he turned around right then? The people didn't seem cannibalistic, not in his dream at least. When they'd seen him, they hadn't attacked, or even gotten up for that matter. In fact, they had been kind. The masks must have been there to scare people off, or *something* off.

The torches that lined the village formed what Hank could only imagine as some sort of barrier. *Why, to keep the darkness out, of course.* The old woman's words echoed through his memory. The barrier was to keep out the darkness. His heart raced. But what was wrong with the darkness?

Everything.

The steps had drawn closer now, he was sure of it.

It wasn't the darkness he had to be afraid of. No, it was what was *in* the darkness. Jennifer's legs yanked out from under her, and then, in the blink of an eye, her body was pulled into the forest with a deafening shriek.

"Hank?"

He looked up, startled, ready to react.

"Hank," Eve said, "I don't think you did anything to Jennifer at all. You're kind. I don't—" She paused for a second as if gathering her thoughts. "I do wonder how you knew where to look for Jennifer's camera, though. Can you please tell me?"

She had fallen back to walk nearly in line with him and was looking down at the ground, down at where Hank's light was shining. Hank looked up to locate George, who he saw was walking a short way ahead of them. Hank was a little surprised that he had taken his eyes off his wife, let alone allowed her to come back and talk to him after behaving as though he was the guilty suspect in a crime he hadn't even committed.

He looked at Eve who then looked up at him.

"You'll think I'm crazy, I think," he mumbled.

"No. I really won't," she pleaded. "Just give me a chance. I really just want to know."

"I dreamed it," he said, quiet enough that only she would be able to hear him.

Her expression morphed into shock and confusion.

"I don't know," he pushed on before she could call him crazy. "I had a dream that—" He paused, considering how much to tell her, how close to the edge of insanity his words could walk before she would immediately scream to the others and call him a lunatic. "Those trees, the formation, I guess, like how the trees looked—it was exactly like I had seen in my dream."

"What else did you see in your dream?"

"Not a lot," he said, picturing the deformed people in his head, and the masks, and the torches.

"Please, tell me," She pushed. "I think there's more, isn't there?"

Scott and Charlie had taken notice of their whispered conversation and were watching now, probably wondering what exactly he was telling her. They knew of the dream as well; they had seen what he had seen. But Eve hadn't. She hadn't shared the dream that Hank had.

"Please."

"There was something in the darkness, in the woods. I don't know what it was." He paused and took in a huge breath. "I think it took Jennifer."

Her eyes widened. "I knew it," she said. "I felt something, like there was something in the woods. I've felt…watched the entire time I've been on this mountain. I never feel alone. There's a presence, or something, I know it."

Hank felt a wave of relief at her not calling him nuts. Maybe she would be an ally if things broke out again. He wasn't sure what was out there, but she felt it, too.

"I agree. I've felt it too, but if we tell the others, they'll just think we're crazy. That's why I haven't told anybody yet."

"Even at the cost of being a suspect." She nodded. "I think I understand. George definitely would—think you're crazy, I mean. Both of us. He already thinks I'm losing it; I can tell by how he talks to me, and by the way he comforts me. A little bit like I'm a child. I'm not sure I like it very much."

"Maybe we should keep it between us for now then," Hank said. "Just for now."

She nodded in agreement, and as soon as she walked away, Scott hurried over. "What did you tell her?"

"Not a lot, just that I had a dream." Scott didn't look like he believed him, but Hank didn't care at the moment. "She didn't have a dream, not ours, at least."

"Hmmm," Scott said. "I don't know."

The footsteps behind him returned as if they had been waiting for Eve to leave. Scott was about to move away when Hank reached out and grabbed his arm.

"Wait," he said, staring straight ahead. "Just— just hold on one second."

"What?" Scott asked.

Hank let silence return, waiting to hear the steps again. A few seconds went by, and Hank thought, for an instant, relief and hope that maybe it was all in his head.

Then they came again.

Hank was almost trembling. "Can you do me a favor?"

The steps thumped behind him.

"Uhhh, sure?"

The steps were so close, so consistent. Whoever, or whatever, was back there, Hank was almost sure it was preparing to strike. The air took on a tense, nearly palpable aura, threatening to choke away his next words.

"Is there somebody behind me?"

Scott glanced back. Out the corner of Hank's eye, he could see the back of Scott's head moving as he looked around.

"No?" Scott said as he turned back around. "There's nobody there. Why?"

A weight lifted. Hank closed his eyes, letting himself return to Earth. A cool breeze rolled by, and he realized he had been sweating.

"No reason." He cleared his throat. "Just letting the dark get to me, I think."

Hank looked up and saw Charlie staring their way like he wanted to come over but wasn't going to for some reason.

"Is Charlie okay?" Hank asked.

"I don't know. He's been pretty quiet. It's not like him."

George glanced back at them with a look. Hank tried not to meet his eyes, which he could barely see in the dark anyway. He wondered if Eve had slipped up and told George what he had dreamed.

"You better go," Hank whispered to Scott. "These guys are already suspicious of me enough without all this whispering."

Scott only nodded and then took a few steps away. But as soon as he did, Charlie swooped in, his turn finally arriving it seemed. Up close, Charlie looked worse. He was shaking a little and fidgety, his eyes wild and red.

"Do you know what's going on?" he asked, glancing in every direction like he was about to sell Hank drugs.

"What do you mean?" Hank asked.

The steps came back. Step. Step. Step. He didn't understand. How could the person behind him have disappeared long enough for Scott to miss him and then just catch back up like that?

"Do you hear it, too? The steps?" Charlie asked.

Hank's head jerked to his side, meeting eyes with Charlie. "You hear it, too?"

Charlie shook his head frantically. "It's in the dark. I've seen it, I think. I've been seeing a lot of things."

"What are you seeing?" Hank asked desperately.

Charlie blinked rapidly, his Adam's apple bobbing as he swallowed. He looked at Hank and then behind him, letting his eyes drift further back than his head, peeking. He was shaking heavily now.

"She's tall." His eyes grew and glistened with water, his words labored, like he was jogging. "And, and she's wearing a black, um, cloak. Her eyes, they're so far back, like—they're like rivers of blood emptying into a black hole. And her fingers are long and thin and…her skin is barely even there. I can barely even see her. It's like…"

Hank was shaking now, too. He felt empty. Like the only thing that mattered in the entire world was Charlie's words and what Charlie was seeing. Icicles of cold air were pricking the back of his neck, raising the hairs. He could feel a sensation, like something was inches away, like something was breathing right on him.

"It's like she's…death."

Hank's light was facing away from the path now, unintentionally toward Charlie instead. The shine hit Charlie's eyes. And in Charlie's eyes, he believed, impossibly, that he could see something, a sinister reflection of something cloaked and dead.

"No," Charlie said, coming to a stop in his tracks. "She's worse than death. She's the darkness."

In a flash, Hank gathered what little courage he had and whirled around, his heart throbbing, his fists clenched with anger, and fear, and sweat. But there was nothing there, only the empty darkness. His heart was pounding so heavily that he feared he may drop dead right there.

Then came a shriek.

But it wasn't the thing, the witch; it was Eve screaming behind them. Screaming only one word that made no sense at all.

Jennifer.

Chapter 13

Eve pointed into the woods, her hand shaking intensely, her eyes darting from the woods, to George, then back to the woods.

"She was there! Jennifer was right there! I just saw her!"

"Eve." George reached for Eve's arm, but she pulled it away violently.

"No!" she screamed. "No! She was right there! I'm not crazy! I'm not! I saw her!"

She looked at Hank as he approached, her eyes overwhelmed with tears. "Hank, you know! There is something out there, something in the darkness, and it has Jennifer! It has her, and she needs our help." She was barely able to get the final words out between choked sobs.

Hank just shook his head, unsure of what to say. How could either of them help Jennifer against the thing that Charlie had just described to him? There was nothing they could do. No way they could win.

"Eve," he managed. "I—"

She's dead. It's what he wanted to say but couldn't. Whatever she saw, he didn't believe even for a second that it was Jennifer. He couldn't prove it, and he didn't know how he knew, but something deep within him told him that there was no way that Jennifer was still alive out there. Not in the darkness. Not with that thing.

She saw his reluctance. It wasn't anger in her eyes, anger that he wasn't standing up for her, anger that he wasn't telling everybody what he had seen in his dream. It was disappointment, maybe even shame, in him and the confidence she had put in him.

She looked upon them all blankly, her cheeks flushed and reddened, her eyes lakes of tears. "It was her."

Before anybody could react, Eve bolted into the darkness. In the split second it took everybody's minds to process what had just happened, she was gone, the patter of her steps digging deeper into the forest. Then, without a word, George took off after her. Jackie almost followed in tow, but Jake, thankfully, reached out and caught her by the back of her shirt.

"No!" Jake shouted. "Don't!"

She turned on him, ready to attack.

"You can't see out there! You'll get lost!"

Hank thought she was going to throw a punch at him, but she just put her hand on him and started crying instead. Scott walked over to where Eve had disappeared into the darkness, standing just at the edge, where the combined light of everybody's flashlights ended. He faced away but then turned back toward Hank, a clear look of puzzlement on his face. But he wasn't looking *at* Hank, but past him, just over his shoulder. Hank rounded to see what had caught Scott's attention. When he turned, Charlie was there, standing not far behind Hank, a peculiar smile on his face. He didn't hide it when Hank saw; he just kept standing there. Charlie wasn't looking at Hank, or Scott, with his smile, or anything else it seemed. He was just gazing off into the distance, a maniacal smile etched into his face.

"What should we do then?" Jackie asked. "We—we can't just—"

"We can start a fire," Hank said, turning away from Charlie with a sort of sickness in the pit of his stomach. "It's getting late anyway." The time on his phone said it was evening now even though it didn't seem like they had been walking for very long. "We can start a fire and camp for the night. If we have a fire, maybe they will see it and can use it to find their way back. It's all we can do."

Jackie nodded, wiping a tear from her eye. "You're right."

As they set up, Hank tried not to look at Charlie because, if he did, if conversation started, he knew he would have to ask his friend why he had been smiling like that. Perhaps it was some sort of nervous tick. Hank conceded that any smile, probably, could look sinister in that terrible lighting, especially lost deep out in the woods.

Nobody needed to say anything. Jackie, Hank knew, was on the brink of tears. If somebody even spoke the word "Eve," he was almost certain she would break down. Jake was, not unexpectedly, staring at him angrily every chance he got. Scott was silent. And Charlie…he wasn't sure what he was doing. And he was trying his best not to know.

Jake knelt and tried starting the fire. Even with lighter fluid, the sticks and twigs fought the flame. Just when he thought Jackie would cave and step in, the kindling finally caught fire. Soon, the larger sticks went up in a blaze. It lit the area, but something seemed different about it, like the range of the flame's light was smaller somehow. As if it were too weak to penetrate the dark or as if the dark had actually grown stronger.

After setting up the tent, they found places to sit around the fire. Jackie and Jake sat on one side, Hank, Scott, and Charlie on the other. Almost like two separate teams. Setting up the tent seemed more like wishful thinking than anything at that point. He doubted very highly that any of them would be getting any sleep that night, not with George and Eve out there somewhere.

Hank wrapped his arms around himself, hugging in an attempt to trap in some heat. The temperature was dropping rapidly. His breath turned to fog as it left his mouth.

"You know," Jackie started, her voice shaking from the cold. "We weren't even supposed to be here. It wasn't the original plan, at least. I got sent home from work because it was slow. And Jake had off."

Jake scowled as if he wanted her to stop right there, to stop telling Hank anything about their life together. The fact almost made Hank smile. It was as if he thought the one thing standing between his life and his death was Hank knowing what their reason for being there was.

"Life had been so hectic lately. We…started to drift a little. Thought maybe coming back here, doing something we both love, could pull us away from our troubles and back toward each other."

It took everything Hank had not to smile when Jake looked at her with such embarrassment but then turned away, hiding his face across the fire. That didn't stop Charlie, though. Hank turned his head to see his friend grinning. But was it because of Jake or was he still grinning from before, or maybe because of something else altogether? He didn't want to know.

"That got us far," she continued.

"I think it was helping," Jake snapped back, not in an angry way, but defensive and timid. "Until we met this asshole, at least."

He shot a glare at Hank. Now there was anger; it was unmistakable. He went to stand, but Jackie placed her hand on his shoulder and pulled him back down.

"Jake! Stop!"

He looked back at her as he sat.

"This is the problem," she said. "I don't know what's come over you lately, but this is you, all the time. This angry person that I don't know."

"You know why I'm angry?" he shouted back at her. "Because you're always complaining that we aren't what we used to be, that things seem different. You want everything to be some perfect fairytale. Well, it's not! You want me to be somebody that I'm not! You think I should be this free, adventurous person that has no cares or stresses. Well, I hate to be the one to tell you this, but the world is full of responsibilities. I don't want to be out here climbing a damn mountain! I want to be home resting because I'm too fucking exhausted! This was my day off, and I was supposed to be laying on the couch, relaxing!"

She just stared at him, not even crying, not angry, just stared; speechless.

His anger sagged into a tired frown. "I love you to death, Jackie, but I don't think you love me. I think you love the person you wish I was."

Without a response, she stood and started walking away. Just then, there was a shuffle in the bushes, then a groan. Suddenly, George came bursting out from the darkness, collapsing to the ground as he entered the light. Hank thought the old man had fallen unconscious, but then his head lifted.

"I couldn't find her!" he cried out. "I looked all I could, but I couldn't find her. She's...lost."

George collapsed back to the ground in a heap. Hank watched as Jackie scrambled to bring him back to consciousness. *Lost*, George had said. Eve was lost. But she wasn't lost in the darkness. No, the truth was much worse: she had been consumed by it.

George woke with a start. He sat up, the nylon crunching under his shifting body. He couldn't see much of anything around him but could make out the fire's orange hue on the other side of the tent's entrance.

He took in a long, deep breath.

He didn't remember much. The darkness felt like a blanket wrapped too tightly around him, suffocating. He tried hard to think, to push through the fog in his head. He had chased Eve into the woods, but it had only taken seconds for him to lose sight of her. The darkness was impossibly black like being lost in an endless pit of tar. He remembered shouting her name but barely hearing himself, as if the darkness itself were sucking up his words and smothering them out of existence.

He'd walked around, his arms outstretched, bumping into trees and scraping against brush. He had lost hope…for her, for himself, for everything, until he had seen the faint glow of the campfire what seemed like miles away in the distance. But he couldn't have walked that far already. It just wasn't possible. He felt like a boat trapped in the tides, drifting against its will further and further away from shore.

He started toward it, knowing, at least for a second, that he could never reach it. It was a star in the sky, only further away. Tears were in his eyes, blurring what little vision he had. He knew that Eve could be five feet away from him and he would have no idea. She could have tripped and fell, knocking herself unconscious. She could be dying, and he would not see her.

All that pushed him was his desire to get back to camp, to make it down the mountain, and to get help. If he made it back, he would insist they leave the tent there. They would just have to go on without it the rest of the way. He needed to leave it as a marker, so he and the park rangers had a place to start when they came back to look for Eve. And if Eve somehow made it out of the woods, she could use it for shelter.

That's if Hank agreed. It was his tent, after all. But he had to understand how much more important it was for them to leave it. That wasn't all he wanted with Hank, though. Before she had taken off, Eve had pleaded to Hank about something he apparently knew, that there was something in the dark. He wanted to know what in the hell that guy had said to his wife that drove her to this madness. What in the world did that lunatic think was in the darkness?

He had started picking up speed, the thought of Eve out there, lost and terrified, pushing him to his limits. The quicker he got back to the camp, the quicker he could get help. Maybe they would think he had given up on her, that he was a quitter, but he had done all he could do. It was impossible out there, to see beyond your own nose, if you could even see that far.

He was running hard. The fire was finally beginning to take shape, a bright light shining through the cracks in the brush. He could hear screaming, the voice of that Jake kid. He didn't know much, if anything, about the guy, but he was sure it was him. He hoped they were okay as he approached, his lungs tired and his legs growing infinitely weaker by the step.

Then he burst out from the trees, his legs caving out from under him as he tore into the light. He saw the startled looks on their faces as he stumbled to the ground. With his last seconds of energy, he cried out for his lost wife, telling them that he couldn't find her, that she was lost. He was afraid then that one of them would offer to go looking for her, but he damned the thought, wanting to tell them that nothing could be seen out there, that they had to stay near the light. But that was where his memory ended, that was when, he remembered now, he had passed out.

He scanned the darkness, his heart rate picking up as the blackness closed in around him. But it wasn't like when he had been out in the woods. There was a fire here, and light. The darkness was not absolute. They must have moved him into the tent after he passed out. For that, he was thankful. He heard snoring and realized the others must have been sleeping close by.

He was awake now. But why? Something had woken him, a sound maybe. He slowed his breathing and listened. Beyond the breathing and snoring of the others, George could hear the fire crackling. A stick snapped. He thought it was the fire at first until something moved loudly through the bushes just outside the tent.

He froze.

"George!"

George would have jumped had he not been ten years out of shape and in a tent. The voice had come from far away, that much he could tell.

"George!"

His heart began to race. He thought it was Eve, the voice, but it was too far away. It could only be her, or Jennifer, but something told him it had to be Eve.

He reached for the zipper and climbed out. The air clung frigid to his skin. He couldn't believe how cold it had gotten, and it wasn't even winter. His breath drifted away in a white, snowy cloud.

He looked around. A dense fog had formed around the peripheries of the camp. He tried to calm himself. He needed the voice to come again. He needed to know which way it had come from, which way he needed to search. But the thought of going back into the darkness had his muscles tightening and his heart thudding.

"George."

He jerked around, to where the whisper had come from, but there was nothing there. It grew colder still, so cold that George wondered how the fog hadn't just frozen over, locking them inside some twisted ice tomb.

"George," the whisper came again, this time from a different direction, as if the whisperer was circling the camp.

He spun around. "Eve." He continued turning frantically, trying to see anything beyond the veil. "Please, just come out. What are you doing? This isn't a joke."

He waited for another haunting whisper. When the next one came, he would just run directly at it. The bushes shuffled as something darted around just out of sight.

Suddenly, it went quiet. The fire died down a little, causing its light to recede. He stepped back, toward the tent. As the darkness closed in, it seemed to undulate, to shift around like an ocean, to pulse as if it were alive.

Then the fire died out in an instant. But not as if it were put out, but as if the light had been deviously stolen away. He thought he could still hear the faint cracking of the fire feeding on wood, like it was still there beyond what he could see. His skin tingled, electric, like ants under his skin. His vision blurred and he thought he was going to collapse.

He stepped back again, toward where he knew the tent to be. It was his only chance. Whatever had been calling to him, it wasn't Eve. It wasn't Jennifer. They wouldn't do this. They couldn't. Right when he was about to make a break for it, something grabbed his arms and pulled him forward. A face broke through the dark, moving in so close to his own that he could see it in blurring clarity as he tried to remain conscious.

His eyes teared in that second and burned with bewilderment, because what he saw then was both horrible and perplexing but also expected. What he saw, what he stared into, standing there alone in the frigid forest of the Adirondacks, were the eyes of something twisted, something deprived and sick. But more than anything, what he saw there was pure evil.

Chapter 14

The scene was very familiar. Hank awoke when the others did, the sounds of their movement pulling him from a strange dream. It faded away the moment his eyes sprung open, leaving only the memory of dense forest and a terrible sorrow in the pit of his stomach.

"He's gone," Jackie said.

"He might be outside," Jake replied, unzipping the tent.

For a split second, Hank almost expected to see sunlight eclipse the opening as Jake yanked back the tent lap, as if the whole thing had been some sort of terrible dream, only that was not the case. Not at all. The first thing Hank saw was the fire, which still weakly clung to life, burning away at what little remained of the wood they had stacked on it before going into the tent.

Hank got up in a hurry and followed out behind Jackie.

"George?" Jake called out.

Jackie turned a full rotation, trying to locate the old man. "George!" she shouted.

The calls echoed off the distant mountains, returning to them only faintly as echoes. Hank didn't bother yelling. The previous days being trapped on that mountain had taught him that screaming out for those lost would not solve any of their problems.

"I don't understand," Jackie said. "He was just here. We brought him into the tent ourselves."

Hank could hardly see Scott in the light of the dying fire. His friend looked worried. Not only was Scott not shouting along with the others, but he also looked distracted, as if something else altogether had his attention instead. Just when he was about to ask him what was wrong, Jake rounded on him.

Jake rushed straight into Hank's face, so close that his hot breath and the stench of being stuck on a mountain for days blasted him right in the face. "You did this, didn't you?"

Hank stepped back. "Did what?"

"Whatever the hell happened to George, it was you. I don't know what you did or how you did it without waking the rest of us up, but I know damn well it was you!"

Hank was about to respond when Jackie cut in, but before she could even speak, Jake lifted his finger toward her, shutting her down. "No! Not this time, Jackie! I know you don't want to believe it, but this asshole has something to do with it!"

The fire sparked up, catching a second wind in the breeze. It colored Jackie's face and reflected off Jake's furious eyes. It lit the indistinct trail they were on and the woods around them. Everything other than them was so silent, so empty and desolate. They could be on an alien planet or the last life on earth.

Jackie looked at him with sad, sorrowful eyes on the brink of collapse. She stepped forward, slowly, looking at the ground and then up at him. The fire danced just to her one side, and Jake stood on her other, with darkness to her back.

"Did you?" she said in a near-whisper, like a child asking a long-lost parent why they left. "Did you have something to do with George? Or Eve? Or Jennifer? Do you know where they are?"

For the first time since this all began, Hank could feel his own tears reaching for the surface. A memory came rushing back to him. Mary standing in front of him after a big fight, the biggest they had ever had, tears in her eyes. She asked him such a simple question, one that did not require any thinking at all yet took him a devastating moment to answer. She asked him if he still wanted to be with her, if he still loved her.

He did, more than anything in the world. But he was angry and wasn't thinking straight, his mind clouded with frustration. He answered yes but only after a long minute, a long minute that, according to Mary, spoke more words than he could have ever said. She wanted the truth from him. She wanted his love.

That was the single biggest regret in his life, not giving Mary the love she deserved while he still had the chance, showing her exactly how he felt, helping her to feel the endless love he had for her, before it was too late.

But it *was* too late. Just like now, here in the mountain forest. It was too late for so many, and there was nothing he, or any of them, could do about it. These two in front of him, they wanted the truth. He knew, though, that no matter what he said, neither would believe him. They wanted someone to blame for the terrible things that were happening to them.

He swallowed hard. "No." He pushed back the urge to cry. "I had nothing to do with it. I—"

"Bullshit!" Jake yelled. "Bull-fucking-shit! You know damn well you did!"

He pushed through Hank, toward the tent, as Hank's eyes locked with Jackie's, both rimmed with tears now. He wanted to repeat himself, to assure her that he was innocent, that there was something else out there, something doing this to them, but his words were choked in the back of his throat. And if he tried to let them out, he was afraid that he would fall apart.

Jake came rushing back toward Jackie, their bags in his hands. That's when it clicked; that's when he realized what Scott had been so distraught by. Hank spun around, taking in the whole campsite. There was something missing.

"He's gone," Hank said, more to himself than anybody else.

"No shit!" Jake yelled. "You're a fucking psycho."

All this time they had been so worried about George being gone that none of them had noticed that Charlie was missing as well. Jake grabbed Jackie's arm and turned her away. Hank whirled around, desperation surfacing.

"No! Wait!" he yelled.

But all Jackie did was glance back, the fire glinting off her tears. She didn't turn around. She didn't ask him to come. She didn't believe him. Nobody did. When he turned back to Scott, he realized that Scott, his best friend, may not believe him either. Scott stared at him, questioning, as if he were unsure if he should have left with the others. They just stood there for a long moment.

"What do we do?" Hank asked. "Should we wait for Charlie?"

"Where do you think he went?" Scott asked.

Hank shook his head, his words unsteady when he spoke. The question seemed almost ridiculous. "I don't know. There isn't really anywhere to go except the woods, and if he went out there—"

Charlie may as well have been as doomed as the others. He knew he should have been sad or something, about Charlie disappearing, but his emotions were so numbed at that point that all he felt was unending hopelessness. He remembered the sick smile that had formed on his friend's face, like there was something amusing about the whole situation. But just before that, he had been terrified when he had seen whatever thing had been behind Hank. Why had his attitude changed so much, so quickly? None of it made any sense.

Even if Charlie had gone off the deep end, pushed there by whatever witch or monster was out in these woods, he would never be able to survive out there. Not alone. Not with this darkness enveloping everything, and the elements, not for long.

"I guess we could wait a little while," Hank said.

He didn't believe that would make any difference, but it was the least he could do for his friend. He would get the fire going whatever little bit he could, and he would sit and he would wait. Scott just nodded and took a seat. He was willing to wager that Scott had the same opinion that he did on how pointless waiting would be. All it did was kill time. But up there on the mountain, time seemed to be the only thing they had, as long as they could stay out of the darkness.

He sat exactly where he had sat before, facing across the fire at where Jackie had once been. And that was where he waited for how long, he did not know, listening to the fire crackle and pop. But Charlie didn't come back. Finally, he stood and grabbed his bags. He wasn't going to bother with the tent. Somehow, he knew that, very soon, he was going to make it down the mountain or he wasn't. Soon, the end would come. He signaled for Scott to come along, they grabbed their things, and then they left behind the campsite one final time.

They didn't speak as they walked. The batteries on their phones were dying. Hank's was at twenty-four percent, Scott's probably even lower. Hank no longer believed they were on any legitimate trail. Most of the land seemed to be level rather than heading in a downward incline as it should have been. He wanted to believe he was getting closer to the base, but logic told him it was impossible. Yet logic held no bearing on anything up there.

Trees towered to each side as he moved through the woods alongside Scott. Hank eventually noticed Scott pitching him the occasional glance.

"What's up? You keep looking at me."

Scott hesitated, diverting his gaze to the ground first and then back up to his friend. "What did Charlie say to you earlier?"

Hank considered the question. "The darkness, he said he thought there was something in it. He said he saw something."

He recalled the description Charlie had given, the long fingers, the hollowed eyes, the black that was the darkness itself.

"Do you think there is something out there?"

The question echoed through Hank's head. He didn't want to answer. The way Scott asked, it sounded skeptical, as if he were questioning the stability of Hank's mind rather than the contents of the darkness.

A light shined in the distance. Hank's heart dropped. Had Jake and Jackie stopped to take a break? If they did, maybe when he caught up, he could talk some sense into them. He didn't think they should split up. It was a terrible idea. The closer they stuck together, the better. Or would they just scream at him again? Would they act like he was a danger to them and demand he leave?

He picked up his pace, walking quickly through the dark, Scott in tow. He would make them listen. "No" couldn't be an answer, not when lives were literally on the line.

The light grew closer. Hank wondered if they could hear him approaching in the quiet. They would be afraid at first, wondering if he were a monster stalking the woods.

"It's just me," Hank called out, trying to give warning as the fire came into full view. "It's Hank. Just give me a chance."

Some shrubbery stood in the way. The fire appeared to be off the path. That confused him, but maybe they were doing it to avoid him. Perhaps they were more afraid of him than he had thought.

He pushed through a bush to the fire on the other side and stared at it in awe. It wasn't a fire at all. It was a lamp sitting atop a short, metal pole. And there wasn't just one but many, all lining the outside of a stone walkway. At the end of the walkway stood a cabin.

Chapter 15

The smooth stones glittered up the path in the light. Like an airport landing strip, the lamps bordered the walkway, glowing brightly. Grass poked up from between the stones, but the blades were short compared to the surroundings, as if somebody had only just recently stopped maintaining the path.

He followed it toward the building. If he found a house at the end, and it was made of candy, then he would turn tail and run, because that's how crazy this was. Whatever this was, it had his skin crawling. It was foolish, he knew, to even follow the path, but something pulled at him, something he couldn't refuse, a siren song in the pit of his soul. He didn't simply want to follow the path; he had to.

The path ended at gravel. Off to one side was a blue SUV parked a few yards from the cabin. He recognized it and would have gone to investigate it had he not somehow known that he could not leave the path. He absolutely had to continue on to the cabin. And so he did. He moved up the wooden stairs and to the door. On the door, there was the number twenty-three.

He knocked and waited but was only greeted by silence. He didn't want to be rude, so he waited a long moment before knocking again, giving whoever was inside time. Then he knocked again, this time a little harder.

When nobody answered, he reached for the handle, slowly, hesitantly, and twisted it. It opened with no effort, as if it were opening itself, willingly and consciously. He stepped through. Beyond the door stood an open living room where two couches sat in the dark, one facing a flat-screen television. Behind it was an armchair with a small circular table in front of it, a book atop the table.

He walked over to the table and looked down at its cover. It was old, with the color fading and the corners worn. But he recognized it right away. It was a novel he had read back in college. *What Dreams May Come*, a 1978 novel by the late legend Richard Matheson. The story of lost lovers, taken by death, and the limits one would go to get back to them. He picked it up and flipped through its pages. It was completely desecrated. Every line had a thick black mark through it.

The pages suddenly began to wither. He dropped the book as if it were on fire. It hit the edge of the table, then toppled to the floor. When Hank looked down, it was gone. He took a step back, wondering if it somehow ended up under the table. It hadn't.

The cabin moaned and groaned with age like a fierce wind was blowing outside, only there wasn't. The air had been still and silent when he was out there. But it groaned all the same, its bones and its flesh moving in an eerie, familiar rhythm.

There was an opening at the edge of the room where Hank could just barely see the top of a staircase. He walked toward it. Along the way, he saw pictures hung up on the wall and on stands, photos of two people, a couple, he thought. They were holding hands in some or kissing in others. Sometimes they were at home, and other times they were out, at beaches or elsewhere. Everywhere, in every picture, they looked happy, though, like they were glimmering. Like they were reliving the best day of their life over and over again. The way she looked at him, but even more, the way he looked at her, was something else, all consuming, all loving.

He couldn't see the bottom of the stairs. They descended into a darkness. He didn't know how or why a cabin would have a basement, and the stairs didn't look like they belonged. They felt out of place. They were formed from wood, clean and glossy, not like basement stairs should be. He turned and took another look around the open first floor. He remembered seeing a second floor from outside but saw no stairs leading upward. Just another thing that didn't make sense. He turned back toward the stairs and took the first step down.

At the bottom, he could see, suddenly and clearly. But when he looked back the way he had come, there was the darkness once again, the same veil he had seen when looking down, only now in the opposite direction.

He looked on with a sort of child-like curiosity. The room he was in now looked almost the same as the one he had just left. There was the two couches and the armchair, just ahead of him, with a table, the same table, he recognized, and a book on it. As he walked toward the table to see if the words were still marked out within the pages of *What Dreams May Come*, he noticed the pictures that were lining the walls. They, too, were similar to those he had already seen. Only they were slightly different as well. In each, the couple was standing in the same locations, doing the same things, except they didn't look glimmering at all.

He looked away from them, almost repulsed, and hurried toward the book and the table. When he picked it up, he froze, stunned. The cover was blank. He felt around its outside, its corners, and its smooth surface. Then he opened it.

Let her go. Let her go. Let her go. Let her go.

It read the same thing line after line. He started flipping through the pages, frantically looking for the end.

Line after line, it was all the same.

He dropped the book. This time, it landed just fine on the table, and nothing happened. It just sat there, its cover open, *Let her go* scrawled across the pages over and over. He stepped away from it like it had a disease. He wanted to get out of there, and now. He should never have gone in. He always knew that, but he let something within him overcome all common sense.

He looked for an exit, but he couldn't see the way he had come. It was as if no stairs ever existed there. Across the room, though, was another staircase leading down. There was no other option, so he headed for the stairs.

How far did this place go down? He imagined descending stairs all the way into hell, staring at the gates of fire, a horned serpent staring back from the other side. He continued down the stairs. Just when he thought he was reaching the bottom, they turned, spiraling downward like in the corridor of a tall building.

They went on.

And on.

And on.

Claustrophobia was kicking in. There were no windows there, only wooden walls that somehow, at some point, morphed into cement walls. He considered turning around and heading back up, but he knew he would never make it. If exhaustion didn't get him, something else would.

The walls began to shake, just like they had upstairs. Everything around him pulsed. Hank grew worried that the stairway would collapse down on top of him. He broke out in a dangerous hurry down the winding way. One trip and he could end up rolling down endless stairs, hitting his head and ending up unconscious, trapped below the surface in some place that shouldn't even exist.

He finally reached the bottom, grabbing the handle and shouldering the door open, falling to the floor on the other side. He breathed heavily, waiting for the stairwell to collapse behind him. But it didn't. When he looked back, the door was gone. He jumped to his feet and felt a wall where the stairs should have been.

Nothing. There was nothing.

Suddenly, a line started slithering down the wall, a crack in the concrete tomb. Only it wasn't a crack at all. It was lifted, protruding like a tube of some sort, like veins in an arm. It ran down the wall, spawning and growing right before Hank's eyes.

They were everywhere, lining the walls like vines. Then they started to pulse. Everything started to pulse. And the walls shook. He stepped away. What appeared to be concrete seconds before was now black and undulating as if the walls had suddenly come alive.

He turned, searching the area for an exit. At the center of the room sat a single dresser, atop it one framed picture. He walked toward it slowly, everything still shaking and pulsing in the background. He shut it out as the image within the frame became visible. He picked it up and looked at it. There, standing alone now, was the woman from all the other photographs. She was smiling once again, about what he could not know. The man was gone. He turned it around and pulled off the back of the frame, removing the picture from within. On it was a date scrawled in italic pen.

There was one more door in front of him. It appeared from nothing. This one had no vines on it nor was it black or pulsating. It was clean and had a window in it. It looked like it belonged at the front of a house, not hidden several stories below the earth.

The shaking of the room picked up speed. It pounded and thudded. Something was seeping from the walls, but Hank ignored it all. He had to know what was on the other side of this misplaced door.

He touched the handle, a cold metal, and twisted it, forcing himself through before something could stop him. His heart nearly stopped on the other side. In front of him were three people, George, Eve, and Jennifer, all strung up by their heads, blood coursing down their slashed-up bodies. He could hear it dripping onto the floor below. Their eyes were shut, their bodies motionless—all long dead.

A figure sat hunched on the floor, facing George's body. It whispered rapidly, the words too quiet and quick for him to understand. Then it stood, its body rising as if from a grave.

That was when he realized that this room was pulsing, too, and perfectly along with his heart. It thudded louder and harder as the figure rose. He wanted to speak, but his tongue was tied, his mouth sewn shut with anger and confusion, but above all—fear.

The figure whirled around. Hank stepped back, nearly gagging. He couldn't believe his eyes. It was Charlie, and he was absolutely covered in blood, as if he had bathed in the remains of their friends. His eyes were wild, that manic grin still etched into his face. He took a step forward, toward Hank. As he moved closer, his entire being began to morph. His eyes sunk in. His skin turned a pale white. His fingers grew in length and thinned to the bone. His clothes dissolved into darkness.

It was no longer Charlie at all.

It was the witch.

He turned to run. Thankfully, the door was still there. He slammed through it, stumbling through the darkness on the other side. He fought for purchase, knowing the dresser should be on the other side, but found nothing. He heard the door creak and close with a click behind him.

He finally gave in and let himself fall. There was nothing there but darkness. But it wasn't cement he felt below his palms as he held himself up against the ground.

He fished in his pocket for his phone. Finding it, he yanked it out, almost dropping it as he did so. He scrambled to unlocked it and then found the flashlight app and clicked it.

The light came to life, cutting through the darkness. He was back on the trail.

Chapter 16

Hank hobbled to his feet, scouring his surroundings for Charlie. Flashes of Charlie drenched in blood, the bodies dangling behind him, fired through his mind. Jennifer's eyes had remained open, slightly, staring emptily down at him as he bore witness to the ruthless scene before him.

He waited, his breaths heavy, but nobody came bursting out from the brush. Perhaps he had somehow managed to lose Charlie in the dark forest. He quickly killed the light; afraid it would alert him of his position.

It took all he had to remain standing. The mounting pain growing within him went far beyond physical. He had brought Charlie there. Charlie…was his friend. And now Charlie was a murderer.

But why? His heart was throbbing so viciously he wouldn't have been surprised if it stalled out. He just couldn't comprehend what reason Charlie would have to do what he did. He wouldn't do something like that. Then he remembered Charlie's words, his description of the dark thing, the witch. Her dark cloak and her eyes. He tried to recall exactly how he had described them. What if it wasn't a witch? What if it was the reaper? Or a demon? There was just no way Charlie would ever do something like this. Whatever it was, it must have possessed him; it must have entered his body and wrapped its sick tendrils around his heart and his soul. It must have taken over.

He wanted to help Charlie, to free him from the thing's grasp, but he didn't know how, and he was on its turf. He felt hunted, like Charlie was somewhere just out of sight, watching him, that smile that he no longer believed belonged to Charlie etched into his face.

He didn't know what to do, not about Charlie, and not about getting off this damn mountain. It was just him now. It was just… *Scott*.

He spun, searching around himself once again. With everything that had just happened, he hadn't even noticed that Scott was gone. It was like back at the camp all over again.

"Scott!" he called out. He couldn't be alone, not again. "Scott!" he screamed.

The shouts echoed back to him. The breeze picked up, drifting between the trees and the leaves like soft whispers, before dying down again. He was shaking, not because of the cold, but because his mind had wandered back to a memory over two decades old. His dad and mom had argued. Them arguing wasn't a new thing, but he could tell there was something different about this time. His father said things to his mother that no person should ever say to another.

For most of his life, it had only been him, his mother, and his little sister. His dad left him. Mary left him. Charlie left him. And now Scott.

There was a sound in the distance, bringing Hank out of his memory and into the present. He listened carefully. It sounded like running water. His heart leapt. If there was running water, it would be heading *down* the mountain. He had read that somewhere, or saw it in a movie, he wasn't sure. But he knew that if he followed it, it would eventually lead to a larger body of water and always, in the end, to civilization. All he had to do was find it and follow it.

He traced the sound into the woods like a canine hunting for drugs. His phone's battery was running dangerously low. A red icon blinked on the screen. He tried to hurry, cutting through the woods, trailing the beam of light. He tripped, the ground covered in broken branches and other debris, but caught himself, then tripped again seconds later, catching himself on a tree. The bark scraped roughly against his skin, and he dropped the phone. It hit the ground with a soft thud and bounced. The flashlight shined up like a beacon, lighting the trees around it and slightly blinding him if he looked straight into it. He raced to pick it up, knowing that every second of battery counted.

The sound was closer. He turned and faced the light back the way he came. He couldn't see the trail anymore. If he was being terrifyingly honest with himself, he wasn't even sure that was the actual way he had come. He no longer had any idea where he was.

He shambled toward the sound; it was the only thing left to do. He felt like he was still being chased even though he had heard nothing other than the water since leaving the cabin and had seen nothing either. He wondered then, his heart racing in his chest, if he was murdered by a witch deep within the woods and there was nobody around to hear it, would his screams still make a sound?

He smiled as he finally found the running water, but the feeling was short lived. It faded as soon as he was close enough to see it. It had to have been a trick of the light, a combination of his exhaustion and circumstance, perhaps even delirium, because the small, maybe foot-wide, trail of water cutting through the forest floor appeared red in the flashlight's dim beam.

He was in the process of hunching over to touch the running water when he noticed another stream just a few feet beyond it, existing in the dark peripheries of the light. He stepped over the first and got closer to the second. They mirrored each other, slicing through the mountain surface like a knife with the soft sound of water running from a faucet.

The red light on the phone blinked again, reminding him that his hope, his chance of survival, was running out of time. He dropped his curiosity for the moment and began following the streams, hoping they would meet at a river. They wound their way around trees and bushes, piercing their way through the dirt and even parting in some places, forming smaller streams that branched off and connected with the other stream.

Then he heard more running water and flashed the light off into the distance. Just barely, the light reflecting off their moving surface, he could see other streams, all of them heading in the same direction at slightly different angles, all of them as red as the first.

He began following the one that ran just inches from his feet, for how long, he couldn't possibly know. Water splashed onto his feet as he stepped into smaller streams, focusing on the path ahead.

His shoes became stained in red. His phone drew closer to death. Ahead, a flicker came into view, peeking through the trees just as one had earlier outside the cabin. He allowed himself to take in a deep breath, releasing it in relief. There could only be so many fires. This one had to be Jackie and Jake.

He picked up speed. The streams began to move in close to one another. The fire grew in size. Initially, he had thought it was a normal fire, small due to the distance. But now, as he drew closer, he knew that to be untrue.

He burst through a tree line into a clearing. His mouth dropped open in awe. There was a large crowd of people ahead, all of them chanting something in unison. The words were drowned out by a piercing ring that grew in Hank's ears, and in his mind, like a wildfire, like a septic infection spreading to every corner, until it was all he could hear and all he could feel.

At the center, where all of the chanting people's attention rested, was a great fire. And in the heart of that fire was a cross turned upside down. A figure screamed out in agony, tied to the cross as the fires licked up higher.

As he edged nearer, the cross's details took shape, forcing him to question his own sanity. It appeared to be shaped from the flesh, and of the skulls, of humans. He could see mangled faces embedded within it, and eyes, and teeth, and everything else sickening. At the top, where the unholy contraption reached, dark tendrils extended upward. They towered, slithering toward the blackened sky, vanishing into the abyss above. It radiated like a spire, as if all the darkness was centered here, originating from this inverted insult to everything that was good.

The words finally cut through the ringing as the chanting grew in volume, the words spoken in some sort of Latin or something.

Hihhs haaa heel. Hihhs haaa heel. Hihhs haaa heel.

Even the trickling of the streams grew louder, the water rushing quicker, the fire growing brighter. The glow cut a dome of light into the darkness. He saw then that there were many, many more streams of red water, all of them coming from different directions, all of them heading toward the screaming victim on the cross.

He had to do something. He charged forward, jetting himself into the crowd. He pushed by people dressed in cloaks, all of them acting as though he wasn't even there. He tripped and stumbled, knocking into some of them, grabbing one of them by the arm to stop himself from falling. As he pulled himself up, the one he was holding onto broke formation, turning to look at him.

It was them. It was the masks he had seen hung on the walls in his dream, the ones belonging to the villagers. As soon as he let go, the masked person shifted its attention back to the fire and continued chanting as if Hank had never been there.

Hihhs haaa heel. Hihhs haaa heel.

The chanting continued to grow to a deafening shout as he pushed through the final layer of villagers.

When he stepped out from the crowd, he came to a jerking halt as if about to step off a cliff. In front of him was a black hole in the ground, a circle of darkness surrounding the fire, surrounding the cross and the victim.

He wasn't sure if he could get across whatever this was. He looked on desperately as the fire reached just inches away from the man's feet. The streams all converged together on the black hole, vanishing into nothingness as they eclipsed the precipice.

The man screamed out again as the flames finally reached him. Hank realized two things suddenly and simultaneously. The man on the cross was Jake. He was blindfolded, but Hank could recognize his voice and see his face clearly enough now that he knew it was him.

An image surged into Hank's head as he remembered Charlie's words. *Her eyes were rivers of blood emptying into a black hole.* He took a step back, staring at the black hole and the streams pouring their existence into it. The fire clung to Jake's pant legs and began spreading up his body. Agony poured from his mouth as his skin blackened and boiled under his clothes.

Hank wanted to help the man, but fear held him in place, its presence like tendrils growing up from the ground and latching onto his feet, burrowing beneath his skin like fishhooks. He turned to plead with the villagers for help, but before he could speak, the crowd parted. At the center of the mass stood Charlie.

Charlie stepped forward, the chanting continuing in the background like the breath of the forest. Hank stepped back, preparing to be attacked. He was all that remained, the only one that Charlie, and the evil that consumed him, had not yet killed.

But Charlie did no such thing. He walked straight past Hank as if he were not there at all. As he moved by, Hank thought, in a fit of fear, that he had seen a dark shadow hovering over Charlie, like a puppet master over his puppet.

Charlie sank to his knees at the edge of the hole and started mumbling too quietly for Hank to understand over the chanting. The fire had now climbed up most of Jake's body. Jake must have been dead now because his screams had stopped, and his head had sagged.

"Why?" Charlie said.

Hank shifted his attention away from the charred corpse, unsure if he heard Charlie correctly.

"Why are you doing this?" Charlie continued.

Hank was about to ask what in the hell Charlie was talking about when Charlie turned his head toward Hank, acknowledging him for the first time. Tears had filled his eyes. Charlie rose. "This can't be happening," he cried out. "Why are you doing this?"

Hank felt a sudden chill behind him. His breathing grew loud as the presence of the witch's blood eyes burrowed into the back of his head. Charlie reached up and grabbed his own face, his fingernails digging into his skin as it started turning to liquid, as if the fire that had burned Jake was now somehow melting the skin from Charlie's bones.

Charlie's mouth opened and let out an ear-piercing scream. But it wasn't his voice that came out. Hank's body turned bitterly cold as if he had been dunked into a tub of ice. A tingle moved across his skin, trailing past his hairs like barbed snakes. Then, like hooks, they dug into his skin and yanked at his flesh.

It was his turn to cry out in pain. He knew what was happening and jerked himself away from the witch's puppet strings. Charlie's eyes sunk in, replaced by the rivers of blood. His face was falling apart, but that didn't stop his lips from curling up into that sickening smile. Charlie struggled toward Hank, his steps weak and shaky. Hank could see the black cloak, nearly transparent, wrapping itself around Charlie.

The chanting was still there, now deafening and all-consuming. *Hihhs haaa heel. Hihhs haaa heel.* The witched laughed, its chuckle whispering from every corner of the forest.

"Hank!"

Hank jerked to the side. On the other side of the fire, he saw Scott. Further behind him, her mouth open in the scream that had come from Charlie's mouth, was Jackie.

"Hank, run!" Scott yelled. "You have to run!"

Chapter 17

He listened to Scott and took off as fast as he could. The witch only laughed louder. And he knew why. She was the darkness. She was the forest. He could not run from her because he could not run from the trees, and the bushes, and the isolation that was all around him. He could not run from the mountain.

But he had to try. He put one foot in front of the other, bolting toward Scott. When he reached his friend, they both turned and ran in the direction of Jackie. She screamed in return and ran away from them.

"No! Wait!" Hank shouted. "Wait! Please! We have to get out of here!"

She ignored him, running faster than he could have imagined her capable. He didn't blame her. All she saw was her boyfriend burning to death on an inverted cross made from the twisted remains of the dead. She would have seen the cult, and Charlie. But she would have also seen him there with them, not sure of why he was there or what role he had played in Jake's death.

Still, he continued to scream for her to wait up. He didn't want to lose her. They had to find a way down the mountain, and they had to do it together. As they left the fire's light, Hank reached for his phone. As soon as he turned on the light, the screen dimmed, and the red light blinked at him. He was down to two percent battery. Soon, very, very soon, he would be without any light at all.

The darkness around him undulated with life. He could feel the forest breathing. He ran with everything he had, knowing that his only chance at living was ticking toward its own death in his hand. Scott was no longer by his side. He must have gotten lost in the dark again. He could only hope that his friend would see his phone's light and come to him. Ahead, he kept seeing Jackie, just barely, at the edge of his light. He called out to her again, but she ignored it, running so fast that she soon disappeared altogether.

He risked a glance back. There was Charlie, his black eyes gleaming off the light not far behind him. Hank ran hard. He could hear Charlie gaining distance behind him. With each step closer, the air around Hank grew colder until he thought for a moment that the air itself may turn to ice.

When the steps were only right behind him, they suddenly vanished. He didn't realize it right away because his legs were churning, and his blood was pumping, as he put everything into taking each step and staying upright in the dark. He finally realized the quiet and looked back, seeing nothing behind him.

He was so tired. He was out of shape and felt like he would collapse. He stopped and hunched over, breathing in heavily, ready to vomit up his lungs. Even though there were no sign of Charlie, his heart continued to throb. Any second, Charlie could lunge out of the darkness. He had to keep going. He had to force himself forward.

Hank stood upright and scanned the area. "Scott?! Where are you?"

A long moment passed. He heard nothing back from the darkness. He wondered if Scott was calling out to him from somewhere else, if the mountain was absorbing the calls rather than echoing them like they should have been. He couldn't just sit there waiting for Scott, though, because his phone was going to die at any second. It was perhaps the worst decision he would ever have to make, but he had to go. He had to leave both his friends behind.

It was downhill. Lately, most of the way had been downhill, which was good because earlier it seemed like even that was impossible, leaving him to wonder if getting off the mountain was even possible.

He had hope now, hope that he would see his family again, hope that he would be able to return to his wife's grave and tell her he loved her. But why had Charlie suddenly gone? Why had he stopped chasing him? It didn't make any sense.

He hurried, glancing back every few seconds to make sure Charlie wasn't sneaking up on him. If he ever made it down this mountain, he was going to change everything. He was going to change his life and how he viewed the world. He was going to stop drinking and get his job back. Or maybe he would move away and start anew. He wasn't sure. What he did know, though, was that he wasn't going to mope, not anymore. He would live his life for Mary. He would be happy, and he would love. Yes, he would love everything like he had never loved before.

If he made it down the mountain. It wasn't likely. He had known that for a while now. Once the light went out, it was over. He pushed the thought away and increased his speed further. He may have been tired, but there was no time for that, because if he didn't push, he would be dead instead.

There was a scream in the distance. At first, he thought it was the witch, and fear surged through his veins. But when the scream came again, he recognized the voice behind it.

It was Jackie.

He sprinted toward the screams. When he found her, Charlie had her lifted in the air with one arm, her back pinned against a tree. She struggled but only faintly, as if she had already resigned to her fate. She whimpered and cried, her eyes glistening with tears. Her face and arms were scratched up like she had taken a hard fall.

She looked down at Charlie and pleaded. "Why are you doing this?"

But Charlie didn't answer. Hank could feel Charlie's grin.

"Put her down!" Hank screamed. "Put her down, Charlie! Right now!"

Charlie didn't respond. He didn't even acknowledge Hank's presence. He lifted Jackie even higher and started squeezing. She clutched at his wrists, scratching and thrashing. She gasped as the airways were restricted further. Her eyes widened and bulged while her skin turned a shade of blue. Hank prepared to charge him, but the struggle didn't last long. Charlie gave a jerk of the wrist and Hank heard an audible snap. She fell limp, and Charlie released her, allowing her body to drop to the ground in a heap.

Hank wanted to cry, but it was as if he had already been sapped of all his ability to feel sadness. Then he heard Scott's voice repeat in his head, *You have to run.*

Without another thought, he turned and ran as fast as he could. There was nobody left but him. There was nobody left for Charlie to seek out other than himself. He heard Charlie behind him approaching at an impossible speed. Hank threw himself into another gear, running impossibly hard. He could feel all his energy draining away with the extreme effort. But, still, Charlie gained like Hank wasn't even moving.

Suddenly, Hank's foot found a crevasse and he tripped. His body flung forward like a rag doll, and he hit his head on something hard. He rolled around on the ground groaning in pain. His head throbbed beyond belief. Pain radiated to every corner of his body, but he stood back up. He couldn't stop.

It was light again. He could see everything. He could see the trees and the grass and, impossibly, the trail. Clouds drifted by overhead, cutting off the sun's light at times before allowing it to shine again. He spun around, searching for Charlie, for the witch, but saw nothing. He listened carefully for the steps that had been chasing him, but they weren't there.

Birds chirped somewhere in the distance as a cool breeze touched his skin. He took in a breath but felt the pain surge as he did so. When he turned around, he saw motion in the distance, something moving past between the trees. His heart started racing again, thinking maybe it was an attacker, but only for a second. It slowed when he heard a sound that was, at the same time, foreign to him now but also incredibly, and happily, familiar.

He heard the sound of traffic. He stumbled down the mountain, stepping over large roots that jutted from the ground like stairs. He saw a car drive by, he was sure of it. Then another! He hurried, ignoring the pain even though it struggled so desperately to force him to the ground.

He arrived at the street, stumbling out into the road. He looked back up at the mountain and saw Charlie. His shirt was bloodless, and he was smiling. Only, this time, the smile had no trace of wickedness in it. It was the smile he remembered. And next to him was Scott. Both of them waved to him.

There was a screech and then a car turned slightly sideways, a trail of black left behind its wheels as the brakes locked, pulling the vehicle to a stop just inches from Hank. A man got out and rushed to his aid, asking him if he was okay. But he wasn't. Another car stopped, and then another.

His legs shook beneath him and he finally, happily, allowed himself to collapse to the ground and drift away.

Mary stood in front of the kitchen, her hands hidden beneath a sink full of water, scrubbing the dishes. Hank was across the living room, sitting on the couch. He considered offering to finish the rest of them, but Mary had barely spoken a word to him since he had gotten home from work. As a matter of fact, she had barely spoken to him in days.

It was probably better that way. It seemed like any time they spoke to each other, no matter what about, it somehow led to an argument. It was exhausting. Some movie was playing on the television, but he wasn't sure what it was. It had already been on when he arrived, and he hadn't paid much attention to it.

There was a crash. Hank shot up from the couch and hurried into the kitchen. A plate lay broken on the floor, shattered into a dozen pieces all over the place. He knelt down and started picking it up.

"Are you okay?" he asked as he put some of the pieces into the garbage.

Mary nodded. "Yes, thank you."

But there was nothing behind the words. They were flat and emotionless, as if she would have preferred he had just stayed in the living room and let her pick it up herself. He nodded in return, but she was already turned around, another dish in her hand. He rose back to his feet with the final, largest chunk of the plate and put it into the garbage.

He stood behind her for a moment, wanting to wrap his arms around her waist, wondering if she would allow him to do so or if she would shake him off. He didn't want to find out because one of those results would shatter him. So he turned away without another word and headed out of the kitchen, then down the hall to their bedroom. There was a television in there that he could watch. Maybe that would free Mary up a little, allow her to relax without worrying that Hank might talk to her.

He laid down on the bed and turned the TV on. Some news program was on discussing Congress, or maybe it was the Senate, he wasn't really sure. He didn't care. He picked up his cell phone and started scrolling through the pictures. A few months ago, when things had first started to really go downhill, he found his old chats on his work computer and took a picture of the one where he offered Mary coffee.

He had considered bringing it up to her, considered showing her the photograph of the chat, but he was afraid she wouldn't care. What was he hoping would come of it? That she would suddenly remember a time when she loved him, a time when she wanted him? He wondered how pathetic that would sound to an outside observer, how desperate it would sound.

It would probably just make her mad. There came a point when two humans had argued so much, and so often, that anything one person did would cause annoyance to the other. He believed that was where he and Mary had reached. Only, he wasn't fully ready to admit it. Now, here, alone in the bedroom, or alone anywhere else, he could talk to himself; he could think about her and miss her. But he was no victim. He got just as mad at her, and just as often. He had worn her out just as she had worn him.

Now this was the aftermath. This was the calm after the storm. As the debris cleared, as the wind settled and the water receded, all that remained was the tattered shells of who they used to be, and the love they used to have.

Darkness came and the day ended. She finally joined him in bed, sneaking into the room quietly, not because she didn't want to wake him but because she didn't want to instigate conversation. He was still awake as she crawled under the blanket next to him and rolled over to face the opposite direction. He wanted with everything in his being to roll over and put his arm around her, to pull her in close and to kiss her.

But he didn't for the same reason he hadn't in weeks. He sometimes wondered if she had the same thoughts and the same regrets, if she wanted to roll over as well, to pull him into a loving embrace and to break down and cry with him. If she did, she didn't show it. But, again, neither did he.

These thoughts continued to spiral in his head for hours until he finally fell asleep. His dreams were restless and unsettling, dreams of trees and of mountains. Thankfully, all of it fled as he woke. When he did, Mary was already up. He could hear her walking around outside the bedroom, passing from one side of the door to the other. She was pacing, he guessed. Finally, she stopped and entered quietly. She whispered his name and asked if he was awake. He pretended not to be. Whatever it was that she wanted to say, whatever had caused her to leave the room and pace outside the door, he didn't think he wanted to hear it.

He would do anything, he knew then, anything at all to keep the love alive between them. He would get down on his hands and knees and beg. He would plead. He would get any job, do anything, not to have to let her go. He would do anything to remind her of the love they once had. He would spend the rest of his life doing this, proving his love to her.

But that would be impossible. Because he knew that this was only a dream. He knew that time was much shorter than he had known then. He knew that what she was going to tell him was going to shatter him into a million pieces.

He knew he would never get the chance to prove anything.

Chapter 18

He wasn't at the hospital for long before it was revealed that Hank had no wounds, that, of all the blood soaking his clothes, none of it actually belonged to him. He tried to explain what had happened, but nobody would let him. They all just told him to wait and to hold his story for now.

He was unsure of what he was supposed to be waiting for until four police officers entered the hall outside his room at the hospital. He saw them periodically looking at him and then the nurse as they spoke to the scrubbed man outside the door. Finally, the lead officer, the one that had done almost all the talking to the nurse, knocked softly on the door, entering then before Hank could even say anything.

"Hi, Hank." He moved to the side to allow the other officers to funnel in. "How are you doing?"

This man knew his name, Hank immediately noted, but he did not know the officer's name. He looked for identification on the officer's being but didn't see any.

"I'm all right," Hank said, recoiling a little against the hospital bed as the officers fanned out into a line.

"I'm Detective Eli Jonas. These are officers Hansford, Erickson, and Welsh."

He was glad then that he had already been given replacement clothes and that he wasn't wearing the old ones, the ones that were covered in blood.

"Hello," Hank mumbled, trying to make eye contact with them but finding it difficult.

The detective began to explain how they would be bringing him down to the station for questioning, all of it standard, now that he had been at the hospital for an entire day and all his tests had come back positively. He supposed he knew this would happen, that there would be questions. He was fine, physically at least, other than some minor cuts and bruises. Mentally, though, he felt battered, as if existing was now a burden and would be for as long as he lived. The fear-stricken faces of those who perished on the mountain still flashed, relentlessly, through his mind like an endless film reel.

Something felt off about how the officers were looking at him. They looked similar to how the nurse did when Hank tried to tell his story as the nurse inserted his IV and tended to him—disinterested, or perhaps something more sinister.

"All right," Hank said, sliding his legs off the side of the bed.

The soreness came back in a wave. He groaned as he stood. When he said he just had to grab his things, swiping his phone off the stand, and the keys to his vehicle, which was still back at the mountain, they allowed him to do so but with what seemed like annoyance. He shoved them into his pocket, and their eyes moved with Hank's hand as if it were infected with something terrible.

Then they waved for him to follow, moving aside so he could walk out the door, conveniently landing him in the center of them all, two of the officers in front of him, the other two behind. He could no longer deny what was happening. They were treating him like a criminal.

None of them said much else until they arrived at the station. Detective Jonas wasted no time in guiding him to a room. The lights in the hallway were poorly lit but inside the room, the lights were bright overhead. The moment he walked inside, his heart sank to new depths. It was just like in the movies, or close enough, at least. There was a table at the center of the small room, one chair on one side and two on the other. What was on the other end of the room, though, was what shook him the most. There was a large mirror taking up a significant portion of the farthest wall. Hank knew, based on the movies, that it was probably a one-way mirror-window; on the other side, more police officers probably stood looking in at him.

"Please have a seat," Jonas said, gesturing toward the lone chair.

Hank said nothing but took a seat in the chair. He took in a silent, deep breath, telling himself that this was standard, just as the detective had assured him earlier. They had to question him. He expected no less. After all the horrible things that had happened on the mountain, they would need to question him.

Hank swallowed dryly, then spoke. "Would it be all right if I had a glass of water?"

Jonas nodded. Not even a minute later, another officer, one of the other three he had seen earlier, came in with a tiny Dixie cup full of water. He wasn't sure why, maybe it was an effect of the room, or the situation, but his throat had never felt so dry in his life. He took the cup from the officer and downed the entire thing in one gulp.

"Would you like a lawyer to be present?"

The detective's question caught Hank off guard. If he hadn't just swallowed the water, he may have spit it up. A lawyer? Another standard question, he presumed, but it wasn't something he had really considered. *Should* he have a lawyer present?

"No. I'm okay." The words came out before he could think much about it. After all, he hadn't done anything wrong, and he didn't even have a lawyer. Weren't lawyers for criminals? He was a lot of things—a drunk, an asshole—but he was no criminal.

Detective Jonas nodded, then set a recorder at the center of the table. "Is it okay if I record our conversation?"

It was Hank's turn to nod. Jonas clicked the record button and then stared at Hank for a long moment.

"What happened up there on the mountain?" the detective finally asked.

"I…I don't know," Hank said, really unsure of what truly happened. So much took place. So many events that twisted and bent reality. "There was something up there. It…it…"

He suddenly couldn't speak the words. *It killed everybody*. It was the truth, but the words clung to the back of his throat. The cat had his tongue.

"I spoke to the nurses briefly. They told me bits and pieces of your…story," Jonas said, not breaking eye contact with Hank.

Jonas didn't smile like Hank thought he may. The story was wild; he knew this. He wasn't sure anybody would believe him. He thought he may get laughed at. But this detective was not laughing, nor did he crack even the slightest smile.

"But I want to hear it from you," he continued. "All of it. From start to end."

Hank wasn't sure what "all of it" was supposed to mean, but he decided to start with the reason why he was there in the first place.

"Okay, well, I'd decided to go hiking in the mountains with my friends, Scott and Charlie, because…well, my wife passed not long ago, and I just felt like I needed to."

Jonas nodded. Hank's eyes drifted toward the glass, contemplating those on the other side and what they would think of him once he told his story. Or perhaps they had already heard all about it from the nurses as well and had already cast their judgements upon him.

"Needed to?"

Hank shook his head. "Yes." It was something he truly had to do, and he wasn't sure anybody who hadn't experienced what he had experienced would be capable of understanding. "When we reached—"

Jonas interrupted. "Is that all who were with you, this Scott and Charlie?"

Hank nodded. "Yes."

"Scott who and Charlie who? What are their last names?"

Hank had to think for a moment, longer than he should have needed to given how close the three of them were, especially as of late.

"Scott Northrop and Charlie Hatch."

Hank scribbled quickly in his pad.

"Do you know their addresses?"

At first, Hank shook his head no, his mind clouded with stress. He wasn't sure he knew anything at all right then. But then it came back to him in a rush, just like their last names. But it didn't matter; they wouldn't find them at home, though. They were gone, lost, somewhere up on that wretched mountain.

"36 East Sullivan, that's where Scott lives. And Charlie lives at 8 Wyoming Avenue."

Moments later, after jotting down what Hank said, Detective Jonas stood, his notepad in hand, and excused himself from the door. He returned to the room just as quickly as they had with the cup of water except Hank noticed that the front page in Jonas' notebook was now blank, meaning he either turned the page or tore it out and passed it off.

He sat, laying the notepad down on the table. "Let's keep going. Was it just you three, then?"

"Yes, just— I mean. No. Actually, we met some others on our way to the top."

Jonas pulled the pen from his pocket and picked up the pad from the table. From the angle he was at, he couldn't see anything he was writing. He wished he could. He considered trying to lift himself a little to see but thought better of it when he remembered how these people had been acting toward him thus far, as if he were guilty of everything.

"Can you please name them?"

"I think, yes. There were these two, um, Jackie and Jake. They were a couple, I think. And then there were these other three, Jennifer, Eve, and George. They were there together as well. We all ended up climbing together."

"All the way to the top?" Jonas asked.

Hank nodded. "Yes."

"And then what?"

Hank fiddled with his fingers, nervous to say what needed to be said. But he had to. He had to tell their stories, those of the people he had quickly come to care about in the minimal time they had together. They were people, decent people, and they didn't deserve what had happened to them. Not even Jake.

"It got dark pretty quick once we were up there, too dark to try and make our way back down, so we decided not to. We had a tent with us, so…we ended up camping there. It was cold and…not ideal, but it was better than trying to climb down a mountain in the dark."

Detective Jonas nodded again, wordlessly, which bothered Hank more than if he would have spoken or asked him questions. It was as if he didn't really care about what Hank was saying. He felt like a child then, explaining to his mother why the cookies were missing off the counter.

Before Hank could continue, Jonas started writing something else on the notepad. "So, you stayed the night at the top."

"Yes," Hank answered, a little annoyed now, annoyed that the detective was making him repeat himself.

Jonas tapped his pen on the table, staring down at his notepad. Then he looked up and spoke as if Hank's story was not only uninteresting but actually interrupting his note taking. "Okay, you can continue."

Hank stared at him for a long second, momentarily considering telling him no. But he knew he had to follow this through. The sooner he got this over with, the sooner, maybe, something could be done, if there was anything. He wasn't sure he believed it possible. Whatever they truly encountered up there, it wasn't something you could just arrest.

"We woke up and it was dark, even though it was morning then."

This put a glint in Jonas's eye, as if these were the words he was waiting to hear. Hank almost thought he saw a fleeting smile. Hank swallowed heavily.

"It shouldn't have been dark, not at that time, it should have been morning, it should have been light, but we thought maybe it was still dark because of the mountain somehow. We knew it didn't really make any sense. We didn't know what else to do, so we decided to just try and wait it out."

Hank paused for a moment, expecting the detective to try and call him out, to tell him his story was bullshit. He knew early on that even if he made it down the mountain, it would take a miracle to convince anybody of his story. When no retort came, he took in a breath and continued.

"When it didn't get light again, we decided we had to get going anyway. We couldn't just wait up there forever. We gathered up our things and started down the mountain. Not far along we saw…"

"When did it get light again?" Jonas asked. "I mean, it's light out now, outside this station. But when did the light come back for you?"

"I'm…I'm not sure," Hank said.

"You're not sure?"

Hank just shook his head, not willing to repeat himself.

Jonas nodded. "Go on, then. What did you see?"

"We came to this ledge on the mountain. Off in the distance, we saw fire. I mean, torches, maybe. There was some sort of town or gathering part way down the mountain."

Jonas's eyebrows lifted, but he still said nothing. Instead, he turned back to his notepad and started jotting. Hank just waited, knowing he had no other choice and predicting that what Jonas was writing down was simply that Hank was crazy.

"We didn't know what it was and didn't really want to find out, so we tried to avoid it."

"Did you?"

"Did I what?" Hank asked.

"Avoid it, the town, or whatever it was."

A pain shot through Hank's head, surging through it like someone had just touched a live wire to the back of his head. He reached back and touched it, thinking for a moment that he may find blood there. But he didn't.

"What's wrong?" Jonas asked.

Hank shook his head, ignoring the question, and continued. "Yes, I think so." His mind was foggy now, and he suddenly wasn't sure what it was he was supposed to be avoiding. So much had happened.

"We headed down the mountain, but things were different."

"How so?"

Hank nearly burst out, "I don't know! They weren't just different! The mountain, it wasn't as it was supposed to be. It wasn't the same way it was on the way up."

Jonas looked curious but didn't question it further. Instead, he went back to his notepad once again. Hank continued on, eager to get this over with, when he was suddenly cut off by a knocking on the interrogation room door.

Hank glanced toward the door but saw nothing other than a quick flash, something moving past the other side of the door's reinforced glass window. Jonas turned, looking at the door as well. From Hank's angle, if someone was standing in the door, he wouldn't be able to see them, not quite. Jonas rose, lifting his finger.

"Give me one minute," he said.

As Jonas stepped away from his chair, the lights in the room flickered, but Jonas didn't seem to notice. He exited the room without a glance. Hank looked up at the light, hearing its soft electrical hum. Perhaps, Hank thought, maybe even more realistically, the lights were old, and everybody knew they were beginning to die. The light went dim for just a second, as if this was its final moments, and then sprung back to life.

Jonas closed the door behind him with a loud clank. Hank was alone then, in the little room with gray walls and a big mirror, a light shining yellow just over his head. It was only a mirror for him, though, he knew. On the other side were people, police, who could see through to him, judging him as a crazy person even though he could not do the same to them.

The lights flickered again. Eyes. He jumped back, standing up from his chair. In the darkness of the room, for the brief second in which the lights had been out, he thought he had seen red eyes searing through the one-way glass, watching him from the other side with a sick stare. Rivers of blood. But when light returned, the eyes did not, vanishing just as fast as they had come.

The room grew colder, reminding him of the mountain with a pinprick chill. The pain in his head was still there, lingering like a cancer. Hopeless. Incurable. Dread crawled up his spine. His heart was beating rapidly despite his internal commands to remain calm. He took in a breath, clinging to it as his eyes remained locked on the mirror. When he finally released his breath, a white cloud of mist rushed out, grappled by the cold. The chill slithered beneath his skin like a stalking viper.

Jonas reentered, startling Hank. When Jonas saw Hank standing there, he remained still for a moment, as if unsure what Hank was going to do, as if he were expecting Hank to make a fruitless break for the exit.

He did not.

After a quick glance at the mirror to ensure the eyes were not there, he retook his seat, telling Jonas he had merely stood for a moment to stretch his legs. His heart pounded so hard in his chest that he wondered if maybe Jonas could hear it. When Jonas sat down, he held a different demeanor. He stared at Hank as if trying to see into Hank's thoughts. It made Hank want to slide his chair back, away from the soul-grabbing gaze.

"Hank," Jonas said. "You went to the mountain alone."

Hank smiled, not intentionally. "What do you mean?"

"Hank," the detective leaned forward. "There is no Scott Northrop. There is no Charlie Hatch. They don't exist."

Hank stuttered, "Yes, they do." Hank wasn't sure what bullshit this sad excuse for a detective was trying to pitch him, but he wasn't in the mood to deal with it, not after everything he had been through. Anger flared up in his chest, momentarily replacing the fear that drove his heart.

"They don't, though. We had the police stop at those addresses you gave us. Nobody by those names live there. We thought that was weird, though. You seemed pretty confident in those addresses. So we called someone else, someone we had already been in contact with since you came down the mountain. Northrup and Hatch are the last names of your childhood best friends, Xavier and Eddy: Xavier Northrup and Eddy Hatch."

Hank's stomach wrenched like someone had just drove a knife into his guts and twisted it with everything they had. He knelt forward, his mouth open, but no vomit came out. He rested then, letting his forehead lower to the table, the cold metal feeling invigorating against his hot, sweaty head. His head pulsed again, that feeling in the back of his neck, and he rose back up.

"No, Scott and Charlie came with me. We stopped at the store. We picked things up. They were there. Contact the stores. Have them check the cameras." Hank thought for a minute, thought as hard as he could, against the fog and the throbbing pain that seem to only return with such vengeance when he needed to think. "The lady that we met on the mountain! Eve! She took pictures. She posted them on social media!"

Jonas nodded. "Yes, we've seen them."

Hank felt caught off guard. He had seen them? That was impossible unless they had already been up the mountain and recovered, at the very least, Eve's body and identified it. But he hadn't even been at the hospital that long.

"Eve Linderman and George Linderman of 14 Cross Drive in Albany, New York." He said their names flat with no feeling or emotion behind the words.

The detective waved his hand, and seconds later, another man entered the room, handing Jonas a folder before returning out the door without saying a word. Jonas lifted the folder open away from him so that Hank couldn't see the folder's contents, a thin manila layer in the way. Finally, he pulled a large, glossy paper out from the folder and set it on the table before turning it around to face Hank.

It was an enlarged photograph. The people in it, he immediately recognized. It was him and the others he had met, Eve holding her camera up in the air for a group photo. They all had smiles on their faces, excited and ready for the adventure ahead of them, all except Jake.

"Notice anything?" Jonas asked.

He stared at it. It took Hank a moment, but when he did, he rose from his chair in a jump. It didn't faze Jonas, though, the man remaining where he sat. Hank picked up the photograph and held it close, eyeing it with queasy confusion. The picture, it just didn't make any sense. The lights flickered again, pulling Hank's attention momentarily away from the photo. He scanned the room, but it was empty aside from him and the detective. Then his eyes wandered, against his will, toward where he had seen eyes in the glass, but there, too, was nothing, only his own reflection.

The eyes in the glass, had his own deceived him? Had he seen things that weren't there? Had his eyes lied to him? He wondered if this was the case again as he looked back down at the impossible photograph. In the picture, Eve held up a camera, aiming it down at the group of newly made friends. Everyone was there, Eve, George, Jennifer, Jackie, Jake, himself…but not Scott, not Charlie. Neither were present in the photo. But he distinctly remembered his two friends standing right behind him when the photo was taken.

"Hank, why did you go up onto that mountain?" Jonas asked again, the same question he had asked earlier, perhaps the most important question of them all.

"I already told you," he said, the picture still clutched, white-knuckled, in his hand. "I just had to.

My wife had passed, and I was having a rough time. I needed a change of pace, that's it."

The lights flickered again, this time repeatedly, before clicking back on with an audible moan, the light brighter than ever, the pain in his head returning along with it. Why was his head hurting so badly? He couldn't seem to remember.

"What's wrong?" Jonas asked, looking around the room, following where Hank's eyes had been staring, toward the faulty lights.

"The lights. The damn lights keep going out and getting brighter," Hank said, covering his eyes with his hands.

"Hank," Jonas said. "There's nothing wrong with the lights. They aren't flickering at all."

Jonas was lying. Why was his head hurting so damned badly? He remembered running down the mountain, Scott by his side. Charlie in the distance, bruised and bleeding, screaming for them to run.

But then he tripped. That was right. He tripped, and fell, and hit his head. Hank remembered Jonas's earlier question right then: when did the light come back? When he fell and hit his head, that was when the light suddenly came back; that was when everything changed.

He looked back at the mirror, at where he saw the red eyes, and stared as hard as he could, trying to, impossibly, see through the mirror to the other side.

Who was there? Or what? Trees. He thought he saw trees there, beyond his own reflection.

Hank jumped back to his feet. This time, Jonas rose as well. "Hank, sit down."

"No," Hank said, his eyes darting from one end of the room to the other. "No. Fuck you! No!"

The door burst open, and the other three officers from earlier came rushing in. But between the men, in the crevices beyond, out in the hallway, he thought he saw dirt on the floor, as if there wasn't a floor at all but ground instead. And trees. And darkness.

"Hank, I need you to sit down right now!"

"No, you're lying! All of this is a lie!" he screamed, stepping back against the wall.

Just as they were about to rush him, to restrain him, Jonas's phone rang in his pocket. The scene froze for a second as Jonas withdrew the phone from his pocket and looked at the screen. Then he held the phone up to Hank.

"Hank, there's someone on the line that I think you need to talk to."

Hank looked at the phone, his heart throbbing in his chest, his forehead drenched in sweat as he plotted his escape from this madness.

"Hank, take it," Jonas said calmly. "You need to take it."

Hank extended his arm, taking the phone in his hand. He looked down at the screen first, at the number that read across, and knew he recognized it. The numbers jackknifed in his head, bringing the pain back to the surface. They lined up, one by one, in the front of his mind until they formed a thought, a face, a memory that had buried itself in the recesses of his mind.

Then he put the phone to his ear. And in the background of it all, he heard Jonas speak, the words muffled and far away but still there, "It's your ex-wife. She wants to talk to you."

"Hank," a woman's voice said softly at the other end of the line. "Hank, this is Mary. They called me. What's going on? What did you do?"

THE END

Note From The Author:

I hope you enjoyed my latest novel, The Adirondack Witch. I hiked there, the mountain in the story, back in 2017 which is when I first came up with the roots of the story. In it, Hank, the main character, battles with his own mind after having lost his wife, only he hadn't lost his wife, not in the way he had convinced himself at least. That's where Scott and Charlie came in, two chunks of his psyche taking form to further feed his own delusions, to further reinforce his new reality. But how far can a twisted mind bend reality? What is real and what isn't? Is anything at all as it seems in a mind consumed by madness?

As Hank burrows deeper into the forest, his mind struggles with itself, a battle of confliction waging underneath the veil. A path to clarity manifesting as a creepy cabin in the woods, a trope that any horror fan like Hank would love to encounter. A cultish village disguising the truth. A witch to shift blame. Layer after layer of fog clouding his mind's eye. Everything seems to be trying to tell him something but none of it clear. But does even an ounce of it exist beyond his own mind, his own version of reality?

When Hank falls and hits his head, is he finally waking up to the real truth? He discovers light, and humanity… freedom. Only, it's not the truth he wants, not according to the police. But even then, even at the end of it all, he still sees glimpses of something that appears to be the witch. Is even the truth actually a lie? When he hit his head, did he wake up, or did he just dive in further? Is the truth just that, or yet another illusion brought on by the witch's evil? How far can the mind wonder, how deep into the forest can it go, before there is no hope of it ever finding its way out?

Patrick Reuman is a medical lab scientist by day and a writer by night. Most importantly, he is the father to a wonderful little boy named Aidan. He has been writing ever since he was sixteen when a school assignment pushed his imagination toward creating his own stories. One day, he hopes to conquer the world but will settle for conquering the literary world first.

Other works by Patrick Reuman:

A Place So Wicked

The Little Runaway

Sin

Insomnium

Sadistic

Infinite Darkness

Other Works:

A Place So Wicked

Fate brings Toby and his family to Black Falls, New York, where the skies are clear and the future is bright. Except at their new home. There is something off about 23 Ripley Avenue. It's a large colonial house, the biggest in town, where the floorboards creak and even the darkness seems darker. Worst of all is the stench, which seems to emanate from the locked door in the basement, the one nobody can get open. It smells of death and decay, slowly spreading from the basement like a sickness. Toby must uncover the truth behind his new home before the death takes over everything – including his family.

The Little Runaway

EDMUND STONE

THE LITTLE RUNAWAY

She escaped one killer only to collide with one even more deadly.

PATRICK REUMAN

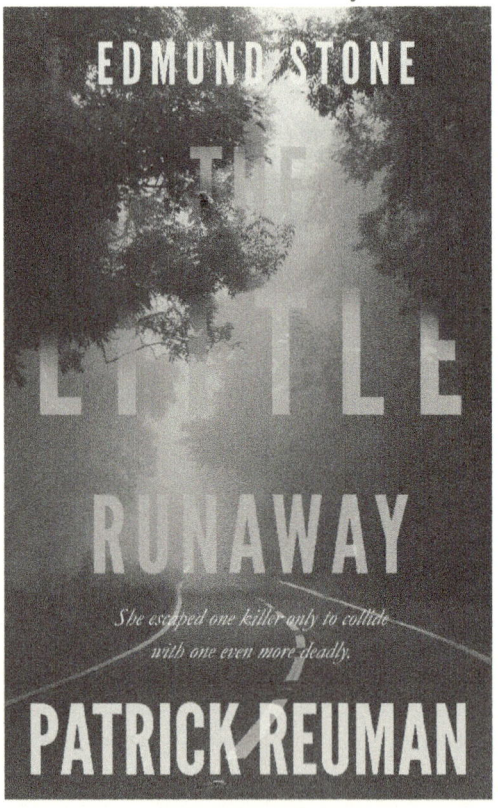

After the tragic death of her mother at the hands of her father, Tera flees before she is next. But on the road, she bumps into an even greater evil. Young girls are vanishing in the city of Silver Creek and Tera believes she may be one of the only people to have encountered the killer and lived to tell the tale. Time is ticking and more girls are disappearing. With her new friends at her side, Tera knows she can no longer run from those that would prey upon her. This time, she will face death head on, and this time… she will.

Sin

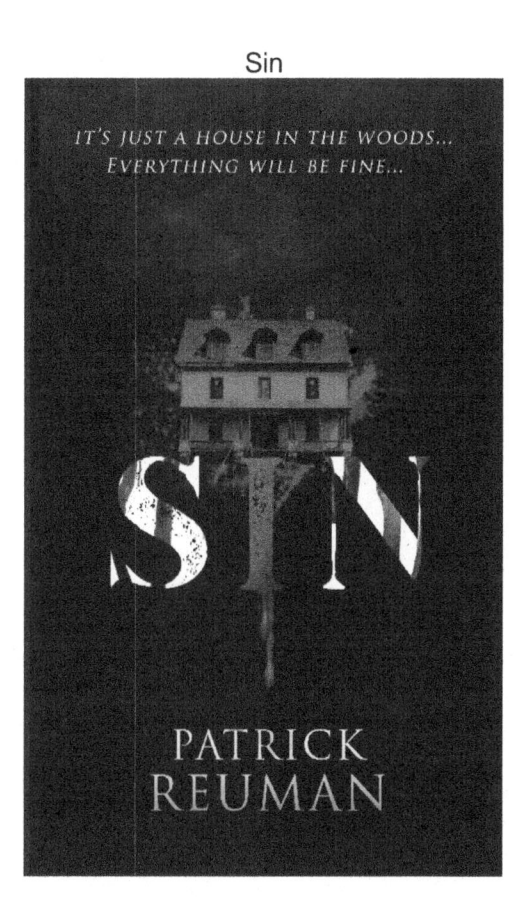

IT'S JUST A HOUSE IN THE WOODS...
EVERYTHING WILL BE FINE...

PATRICK REUMAN

Ryan's relationship is already on the brink when a woman goes missing in the small town of Bakerstand. With the whole town on high alert, he refuses to let this dead city kill what's left of his relationship. But a house in the woods may hold a deadlier fate than the town ever could.

Made in United States
Orlando, FL
12 February 2023